About the author

Annelies Verbeke is a ˅
essays. She is also a screenwriter and a playwright. She
made her literary debut in 2003 with the much-lauded
novel *Slaap!* (Sleep!), which sold over 75,000 copies and
was published in twenty-two countries. Verbeke makes
regular appearances on national and international
stages. Her books have won her numerous awards and
nominations; *Assumptions*, a collection of short stories,
was nominated for the BNG Award. Her work has been
compared to that of Katherine Mansfield and Wells
Tower. Verbeke lives in Ghent, Belgium.

About the translator

After finishing her studies at the University of Man-
chester, Liz Waters worked for some years with English-
language texts and at a literary agency in Amsterdam
before becoming a full-time translator of literary fiction
and non-fiction. Authors whose books she has translated include Lieve Joris, Jaap Scholten, Luuk van Mid-
delaar, Douwe Draaisma and Geert Mak.

Assumptions

Bruges, April 2017

Annelies Verbeke

Assumptions

Translated from the Dutch
by Liz Waters

World Editions

Published in Great Britain in 2015 by World Editions Ltd., London

www.worldeditions.org

Copyright © Annelies Verbeke, 2012
English translation copyright © Liz Waters, 2015
Cover design Multitude
Image credit © Mark Hooper/Getty Images

The moral rights of the author and translator have been asserted in accordance with the Copyright, Designs and Patents Act 1988

First published as *Veronderstellingen* in the Netherlands in 2012 by De Geus BV, PO Box 1878, 4801 BW Breda

British Library Cataloguing-in-Publication Data
A catalogue record for this book is available on request from the British Library

ISBN 978-94-6238-029-5

Typeset in Minion Pro

The translation of this book was funded by the Flemish Literature Fund (www.flemishliterature.be)

Flemish
Literature
Fund

Distribution Europe (except the Netherlands and Belgium): Turnaround Publishers Services, London
Distribution the Netherlands and Belgium: Centraal Boekhuis, Culemborg, the Netherlands

'The light grows slowly like our hair.'

TOMAS TRANSTRÖMER (translated from the Swedish by Göran Malmqvist)

Contents

On Guard Here

Father,

That I'm writing to you says enough. I'm not doing too well, Father. You know that. Perhaps you predicted it. You may even see it as a test. I realize there's no point in writing these words; you read my thoughts as soon as I have them. There's no address to which I can send this letter in its tangible form and I'd be ill-advised to save it in a computer memory regardless. So see this as a prayer. I'm clutching at it as a last possible source of consolation, however much effort it takes me to hit the right keys and however fearful I am that one of my guardians will catch me at it.

Still, that anxiety is probably baseless. If they found me sitting at this monitor, typing, they'd no doubt immediately come up with some explanation that fits what they think they know. Stories. They're good at those. The times when they caught me reading that's exactly how it went. Not that they've caught me reading too often. It's rare to find a good book in this house. He's a complete idiot. I'm supposed to love them, Father, but he's a jerk. He has his tender interludes, but they're no compensation. She occasionally brings in something she ends up not reading. As on all other fronts, resolutions are as far as she gets. She recently decided to immerse herself in Rilke and left two of his collections knocking about in the lounge for a day. As I recall you're no great fan of the poet, you don't find him life-affirming enough I suppose, but as soon as they were out of the house I devoured his lines; as I said, I'm not doing too well. Loneliness, Father, is like the rain, and I can't quote any more than that—I hadn't memorized many lines before they yanked the collection out from under my nose. Tssk, they say. 'Tssk,' Father. And now Rilke is all on his own on the top bookshelf, where I can't reach him.

This is solitary confinement. A prison. He never takes me out, it doesn't even occur to him. As a rule she cares about nothing but herself—shockingly negative, she's sure to come to a bad end. Yet she does sometimes take account of my needs. On occasions I even think she appreciates me and I too have my good moments, my little breathing spaces in this vale of tears, there at her side. If I lay my head in her lap she'll stroke it absently, and even when I shove my nose between her buttocks in a regressive outburst she doesn't get angry. Yes, Father. Regression. Between her buttocks. I can't say it often enough: not doing too well.

There's a question that haunts me, Father, a question that keeps me awake or makes me whine in my sleep. Before I ask it I want to remind you that I've never had any qualms about your decisions before. I really gave all I had to give during your previous initiative. I'm convinced you've not once had grounds to reproach me for a lack of team spirit or personal motivation. I never even complained about the post-traumatic stress disorder that first attempt left me with—for all your omniscience, it's probably news to you.

I believed in what you were doing, what we were doing. But then I was a man, a human among human beings. And I understand why you wanted to take a different approach the second time, I really do, it's a rationale I comprehend and endorse. Like you, I was disappointed by the result last time round and I can understand that you thought: all right then, let's take a risk, let's go for a surprise offensive. But why a dog, Father?

There's no doubting the special bond between human and pet, but surely it's not enough, surely it's no recompense, no ticket to Salvation? What do you expect me to do? Perform miracles? Foster a world religion? Become the main character in the greatest best-seller of all time again? I barely get out!

And now that I've had the gall to ask for an explanation, here's another question: if I must be a dog, why a schnauzer? I have infinite admiration for all the fauna you've created. Each creature is beautiful in its own highly individual way and it's breathtaking to discover how they all slot together like pieces of the most ingenious puzzle. Yet it seems obvious to me that every living being, simply by existing, places limits on the practicability of expectations. That was your opinion too until recently, wasn't it? Your plan? Otherwise it would soon all be over for the Almighty, right?

I find it so hard to believe that you still haven't recognized the fact that the form in which you've sent me to earth is incompatible with what you wish to achieve, Father. As a schnauzer I really am subject to too many limitations. It's hard for me to have to expound upon something so absurdly obvious. I'm short-sighted but not blind. During those rare walks I notice how the German Shepherds and Dobermans look at me. At best they think I'm a sweet little boy-dog. Why a schnauzer, Father? For all the hallucinogenic substances this planet has to offer and for all the insanity that prevails here, no living creature would feel the slightest urge to seek salvation at my hands. I have no hands, Father. This keyboard is already covered in scratches.

The mystery of your ways has cast me into the deepest gloom. Which isn't exactly helping me to behave convincingly as a canine. I wonder how you would react if they put a biscuit on your nose and forced you to sit still. Shake a paw, Father? The days are long and monotonous, the food atrocious. When we're outside and she lets me off the leash for a moment it's not too bad; I pep up and my happiness makes me forget that I was determined to take the first opportunity.

What I'm going to write next is terrible, Father. You're my darling daddy, I've always looked up to you, I want you to be proud of me. If I disappoint you, I disappoint myself; if I hurt you, I hurt myself. Your choice of a schnauzer is so ridiculous, though, that in my gloomiest moods I suspect you no longer care what becomes of humanity. That you think: I've done enough, let them get on with it. I could sympathize with that, in fact I'd even welcome a desire on your part to take things a little easier. What gets to me is my role in all this. If you've given up, then why send me here in such a stupid guise? Is this a joke, Father? An experiment? Or did you want to be rid of me?

The other possibility that occurs to me is—and on this point I suspect you'll agree—even worse. There are times when I wonder whether you exist at all, whether you might just be a figment of my runaway imagination, a delusion that's convinced me I'm a helpless saviour. Do I even exist myself, Father? Is this a lounge, are my owners real? Am I the hallucination of someone locked in a stinking white room, barking like a dog, confounding all diagnoses?

If you exist, you'll punish me for what I've just written, but with all due respect and in the hope that you won't interpret what I'm going to say next as a provocation: no matter how you make me pay for this, nothing could be very much worse than the frustrating dog's life I have now. Don't forget that I've got the horror that befell my previous manifestation to compare it with.

Make sure I quickly come to regret the tone these words convey. It'll mean that I feel you in my heart again, that I know why I'm a schnauzer, that you are there watching over me and I'm on guard here. For you.

Until then I'll go on waiting for a sign, an answer. I'll look forward to the day when you call me to you and everything will be clear in the light of your love. But perhaps my despair will take the first opportunity to get the better of my hope.

Forgive me, Father, for I no longer know what to do.

Your Son

Henny Verhasselt's Life's Work

Henny Verhasselt hovered a fragile, brimful glass of Cava over the heavy tablecloth and tried not to look at Josephine.

'It may sound strange now,' he began, 'but even as a child I wanted to specialize in supplying decorations to the catering industry.'

'That's nonsense, Verhasselt,' said Josephine. 'It would be great if your business was your childhood dream. Especially now that we're celebrating its thirty-fifth anniversary.'

Henny tried to suppress the fluttering of his right eye. He failed and sensed that his son had noticed the tic. He mustn't worry the boy. Josephine was Martin's wife, he needed to bear that in mind. Martin had said so himself—that he needed to bear that firmly in mind.

'But I did,' said Henny. 'Laughing polystyrene portions of chips, bigger than I was. Plastic mussels. Even as a child I couldn't get enough of them. I can show you photos.' His fluttering eye sought his assistant Brigitta, his rock, responsible for transport, who disliked eating out but did it all the same, for him.

Brigitta put down her glass, leaned back a little and concurred. 'That photo with the plastic sausages round your neck.' Her right hand circled her own neck, then indicated how small Henny was in the photo and finally fell exhausted into her lap. 'On the wall out there,' she sighed before turning her attention to a vast inner Nothingness that seemed to afford her immense serenity. It wasn't the first time she'd made Henny think of power tools. Safe electric power tools that automatically disconnect when a short circuit threatens.

'It wasn't a childhood dream,' Josephine impressed upon her father-in-law with a kindly smile. 'This is just life, Verhasselt. Chance. It's important for you to realize that. Pure chance brought you here. To the top of a company selling catering decorations. There's nothing wrong with that.'

'No, of course there's nothing wrong with it!' He hadn't quite shouted, but it was definitely too loud. His son looked stern. Josephine put on her most anxious mask. The glass in Henny's hand had roughly the same diameter as her eye sockets.

She had seemed so different, Josephine, at the start. A clever lightweight possessed of a vision. With a coquettish tread she'd walked into his life to put an end to his son's bachelor existence. She immediately mutated into a business partner, who with breezy insouciance got the company's profit margin growing again. By launching substantial discounts at the right moments, she'd managed to create a hype around a 210-centimetre hotdog that squirted ketchup over its own head, and a waste bin in the form of a flute with scoops of brightly coloured ice cream. Henny saw them everywhere, even abroad. Yes, Josephine had a natural instinct for business. And he admired that.

So he told himself it was perhaps a little odd but certainly not a bad thing that his daughter-in-law addressed him by his surname. No one had done that since primary school. It felt impersonal, but he could no doubt safely assume that Josephine was just being chummy. The way her face creased when she spoke to him might have come across to a less positively inclined person as falling somewhere between impatience and pity. Fortunately Henny knew better.

The fact that she called the classification system he used for his book-keeping 'the work of a psychotic neurotic' and his absent-mindedness 'an infantile expression of unprocessed grief' was another thing Henny was able to live with. It made sense: she'd spent a long time studying these things, far longer than he had; she was more of an expert and she might even be right. Perhaps he was indeed a psychotic neurotic who expressed his unprocessed grief in an infantile way. The thought made him a little nervous.

Josephine treated his son rather fiercely, he felt, but Martin never seemed to detect anything humiliating in the categorical imperatives she deployed to spur him to action, or her frequently repeated remarks about balls, about Martin's lack of them and, very often, about how you needed to have them and it was fortunate she, metaphorically, did. Since he kept forgetting what 'metaphorical' meant and no longer dared ask, every time she talked about those metaphorical balls Henny visualized her with a pair of metal testicles in an odd colour. He knew that every relationship is different, that you can never tell exactly what goes on between couples and that therefore you shouldn't intrude with judgements or helpful advice. Perhaps his son liked the fact that she treated him that way, maybe it had to do with some unconventional kind of sex. It was not something a father ought to meddle with, even if it stung.

The nervous tic had manifested itself only after Josephine arranged for the magnolia to be felled.

He'd planted the tree in the middle of the five square metres of soil next to the entrance to his newly founded company, a young sapling that would grow along with the business. His wife had loved the magnolia. There came a day in April when they breathed the outdoor air together for the last time, when both his shadow and the shadow of the magnolia bowed fraternally over the bony body in the wheelchair. 'In flower,' she'd said with emotion, too much emotion, and he'd answered, gasping for breath, 'There's a lot those doctors can do, Annet.'

Martin had completed the job while his father and Brigitta were delivering an Elvis replica to a seaside bar. When he saw the freshly cut stump, an image flashed through Henny's mind of his wife lying on the ground, alive but helpless, thrashing limbs amputated at knee and elbow. He stormed into his office and caught Martin hiding the murder weapon behind a stack of files. His son, the glove puppet, dropped the saw when his father pointed to it and looked round, startled, at his ventriloquist wife who carried on rattling the keyboard with acrylic nails.

'That tree made too much mess,' Josephine explained through Martin's mouth, lips barely moving.

'It's time for you to let Annet go, Verhasselt,' she had the audacity to add on her own behalf. As if she'd known Annet.

There was suddenly a great deal Henny wanted to say. 'Gob' and 'cunt' and 'out' thundered across the floor towards him and up his legs. Although he felt the words pounding relentlessly in his throat, he didn't manage to articulate them. Only his eyelid excited itself. He stayed in his storeroom for a long time, between two Indians and a cowboy ordered by a client with a steakhouse called Wild West. He would deliver the threesome in person shortly. This was a normal day.

In the months that followed, Henny failed to rid himself of his rage. When he discovered Brigitta crying behind a fern in the showroom—Josephine had condescendingly ascribed to her both bulimia and a mild form of autism—he made a fresh attempt to outline his grievances.

He went over to stand in front of her desk and said: 'There are things in life besides polystyrene, Josephine.' He'd spent a lot of time thinking about that sentence.

'Hmm?'

She keyed in a phone number and leafed attentively through a diary. He yanked the receiver out from between her shoulder and ear, unintentionally tugging one of her blonde locks in the process. She screamed.

'Sorry,' said Henny, and then: 'There are feelings, too, Josephine. People have feelings.'

Now he could plainly see how cunning she was, how evil her intentions were.

'Verhasselt,' she said, the flat of one hand pressed to her temple as if to a gaping wound. 'I think it's high time we sought professional help for you. Don't just stand there, Tin, take your father into the showroom and sort this out.'

'Brigitta never cries …,' Henny began. He trudged off silently behind his son. Martin was going bald, he noticed. His baby scalp had been exactly that shade of pink.

'You need to remember that Josephine's my wife, Dad.'

Martin's voice echoed across the showroom with the force of conviction, but the word 'Dad' disappeared in a sob. He knelt down in the blast of sun falling through the skylight, behind the fern where Henny had earlier found Brigitta, head in hands.

'What is it, son? What's going on?' It was far worse than he'd suspected, Henny realized. It all started with Josephine and led right back to her.

Martin shook his head and, moaning, allowed himself to be helped to his feet.

'I'll sack her,' said Henny.

'Then I can't stay. She'd never accept it. You need us. The company needs us.'

It struck Henny that his son had already turned the idea over in his mind more than once.

'Leave her!' This time he had to be the one issuing commands.

'She'll destroy me, Dad!'

'Or … we her.'

They looked at each other, Henny timidly, although with a fixed, wide-eyed stare, Martin incredulous. Until Henny laughed as if it had been a joke.

'You always need to bear in mind that Josephine is my wife,' Martin repeated, before stumbling away from his father and the fern.

Henny thought about that again later. While stacking crates of ostriches dressed as butlers, for instance. Each was a 190 centimetres tall and around fifty kilos in weight, and there was Josephine, walking heedlessly beneath them.

But. Well.

In the restaurant he looked pensively at Josephine, then at the glass in his hand. It was only when he lifted it higher into the air that it occurred to him what he wanted to toast.

'I've decided to retire,' he said. 'This is the time to pass on responsibility to my son.'

He refrained from congratulations.

While draining his own, he heard three glasses being returned to the table.

The bubbles invigorated him. It was as if they were waking a new, bigger man, one who slowly stood up and, before anyone could put a name to him, made a dash for his freedom.

The Bearded Lady

Just as no one can combat the greying of the population by dying their hair, so Emmy Debeuckelaer could not keep her sorrow at bay by giving herself a good shave. At the age of about sixteen, when the beard started growing, she'd still been able to deny it a public outing. She shaved in the mornings before leaving for school, where she shut herself in the toilets with a pocket mirror and a Gillette in the afternoons. Contrary to her intentions, she was thereby ensuring that within a few months the excessive down would turn into tough, ever-present stubble. No matter how great Emmy's abhorrence of the role, she became the Bearded Lady.

Other than that she had an extremely attractive body, which led some of her classmates to put a sexual proposal to her. The scene they had in mind would be played by six actors and a young woman wearing a mask. Emmy declined the offer and was considered ungrateful. Harassment followed, certainly, but more often she was avoided. They did look, boys and girls, women and men, they looked all the time, some biting their lower lip, others horrified, and all with the curiosity with which people witness natural disasters, just before running to safer ground. Deeply hidden in all those eyes was something else, too, something that was ignored because no one could say quite what it was.

Emmy was not the sort of woman who could easily put facial hair out of mind. Before the beard she'd looked forward with confidence to the moment when she would take over her mother's sunbed emporium and develop it into a fully-fledged beauty parlour. Her mother consulted doctors, who prescribed Emmy pills and injections that didn't help. In the end mother and daughter decided, hugging each other in their affliction, that a beard would not be good publicity for the business, and that Emmy's start, like the new investments, would have to wait for the medical life-raft that was no doubt already being inflated in some laboratory or other and would float their way in the future.

Whole newspaper supplements are printed to convince you that your furniture tells you who you are, that you are what you eat. Lies, all of it, Emmy Debeuckelaer knew. She was her beard.

Although she continued to place her hopes in science, she found it increasingly hard to deny the existence of God. Not so much because she believed that a noble divinity lay behind every ray of sunshine, but rather because she found the idea of punishment more plausible than sheer bad luck. Her beard was a punishment. But for what? She couldn't recall any great personal crimes that would justify such inexorable retribution. She therefore persuaded herself of a previous life full of wild atrocities. A psychic confirmed that suspicion. The clairvoyant discovered that Emmy had been a warrior in the Hundred Years' War, first on the side of the House of Valois, later as a mercenary by the name of Richard the Slayer, deployable on all fronts, ever intent on the satisfaction of his perverse and extremely bloodthirsty destructive urges. Emmy had thought it was something like that.

The discovery of her previous existence at first mainly changed the nature of Emmy's dreams. She'd previously experienced in them a repeat of the humiliations of the day, or had become in sleep her ideal self. Smooth-cheeked, regal hairstyle in the wind, at the head of a Japanese-style beauty salon—the most successful in Europe—she was surrounded by admirers saying she smelled nice, praising the softness of her moonlit skin. In her new dreams her broad fingers clasped an axe. Her muscular arms, all blood, earth, and sweat, lifted the thing above her head time and again and brought it down with full force, right the way through a fourteenth-century village.

At the start Emmy would never have admitted it to herself, but waking from this kind of dream was just as disappointing as from the one about smooth cheeks.

That she had taken on a different guise and was living in a different time from Richard the Slayer did not absolve her of responsibility. She alone could make amends for the centuries-old guilt and get a beardless life in return.

Good things come to good people, thought Emmy. She retrained as a nurse and was able to start even before graduating. The care sector was understaffed, overburdened, and underpaid; a nurse with a beard was, as a consequence, no problem. At least, that was the theory. One little old man had an anxiety attack every time she walked into his room on night duty and two other patients brazenly asked her whether she was undergoing gender reassignment. There were people with empathy and people with advice. The ones who annoyed Emmy most of all, however, were self-declared fellow-sufferers.

The patient in room 432, for example. Emmy couldn't remember her name, probably because after each encounter her brain purged itself as thoroughly as it could of all trace of the woman. Her tragedy was that she'd come no closer to modelling work than a vegetable-slicing portrait on the side of a kitchen shop's delivery van. She'd made reference to it in every conversation before realizing it wasn't enough and never would be, that there wasn't even any such thing as enough.

While the woman griped, Emmy looked with a smile at the clouds, which disappeared more rapidly than normal behind the window frame, as if they felt trapped, vicariously embarrassed by the sight of her beard. The frustrated model considered her a good listener.

Her obese colleague Caroline was likewise drawn to Emmy time and again by an assumed kinship. At least once a week she enumerated all the forms of discrimination that had befallen her, all the ways fat people were disadvantaged by society. The Bearded Lady again showed herself to be a benign listener, who never strayed into making comparisons, never said that fat people should simply eat less whereas for unwanted facial hair there was no remedy. She mentally christened Caroline 'Calorine'.

In her dreams Emmy was less accommodating. As Richard the Slayer she kicked in doors to houses where Calorine, the failed model, the little old man who was afraid of her and all the tip-givers, sympathizers and tormentors that had presented themselves in Emmy's life were hiding beneath rotten floorboards. They wore fourteenth-century clothes and held their breath. Richard the Slayer would walk through the room with a heavy tread, smash some furniture and curse threateningly to himself, as if incensed by the empty house. After stamping resoundingly to the front door, he would open and shut it without going out. As soon as the first sigh of relief rose from the floor, Richard stormed at it with his axe. A massacre later, Emmy would wake feeling relaxed.

All the same, when she then looked at herself in the bathroom mirror—the thing was indistinguishable from the rest of the bathroom fittings—she immediately lost heart. She was a woman with a light-blue silk dressing gown and a full beard that seemed to be growing more and more rapidly.

Since her good deeds as a nurse clearly weren't sufficient to atone for the guilt of her previous life, Emmy decided to take a voluntary job at a shelter for the homeless on her nights off. Now and then there were fights, but usually it was quiet. A schizophrenic woman kept phoning her up with a knitting needle she'd pushed through one of her dreadlocks. Somewhat shocked by the size of the holes in the social safety net, Emmy pressed the three middle fingers of her right hand to her cheek so that thumb and little finger formed the ends of a receiver.

'Don't worry,' she whispered to her finger. 'I'm here to show you that it could be worse.' She initially felt ashamed of saying such a thing, but when the woman, after a slight delay, burst into assenting howls of laughter, Emmy suspected she'd spoken the truth. She would happily change places with the bag lady. Better hopeless than bearded.

She wondered whether she in turn could find comfort

from individuals who had suffered even worse punishments. She went in search of pictures of people put on show in those long-abolished travelling circuses, or in cabinets of curiosities. Hiki, the scaly man from Nebraska. Stella Blanchea, the woman with a tail. Betty Williams, who had the misshapen limbs of a twin sister growing out of her side. The Sanders family, with their leopard skin. Even hairiness could be worse, as proven by Krao, the 'Missing Link Girl' from Laos, whose entire body was shrouded in a coat of fur. 'One of us, one of us,' the photos chanted. Emmy belonged with them, just as a person belongs with his or her family, inextricably bound to them without having chosen to be. Emmy didn't believe that their success and the money they made from their handicaps had made them happy. In fact she became all the more convinced that the world she belonged to was peopled by a sad troupe, a vanload of weeping clowns, however broad might be the smile into which the armless among them inserted a cigarette with their toes.

Did love bring Emmy consolation? Hardly.

At the hospital Bart, a urologist, courted her. He stayed the night ten times or so and came out with wise generalities about mankind such as: 'We humans are certainly the only creatures afraid of death, yet compared to us, animals are free of an even greater fear. The fear that governs us from our first breath to our last sigh is above all the fear of sorrow. An entire lifetime spent worrying about missing out on happiness—and then you die.'

The fact that as he spoke these words a breadcrumb clung to his forehead so endeared Emmy to him that she briefly abandoned her reticence.

He never said anything about her beard and Emmy had to accept that. But after a few weeks she started to get the uneasy feeling that his ignoring the beard seemed to insinuate that she too had largely escaped Bart's attention.

One day, while shaving, she snapped at him that he needn't act as if it didn't exist.

'As if what doesn't exist?' Bart asked impatiently. He wanted to leave for a party.

'Stop play-acting. You're making us both ridiculous.'

He stared at her in exaggerated bewilderment.

'Your girlfriend is shaving her beard. Don't you find that strange?'

Bart shrugged. If he said now that he didn't see her beard she'd be furious with him.

'I don't see that beard,' he said.

After she'd been furious with him, and he'd asked himself in a very loud voice what he'd been supposed to say, repeated that he loved her and to her dismay even resorted to pleading, they decided to give the party a miss, rapidly downed a bottle of Cointreau between them and ended up between the sheets. There she asked him whether she could scratch him really hard, since he struck her as someone she wanted to have under her fingernails and she also asked, sounding far more fragile now, far deeper into the night: 'If at the end of your life you've been hurt more than you've hurt others, does that make you a loser?' As an answer he hugged her until the next afternoon.

It seemed a harmonious time between Emmy and Bart, but you never know what other people are thinking. Even if they say something exactly the way you once put it, it's hard to believe they mean the same thing.

Rather unexpectedly he said he had trouble dealing with the mistrustful way she approached other people, her misanthropy. She described that allegation as deadly, saying her reticence towards others was less now than it had ever been. More arguments followed about her beard, how he dealt with it, how she dealt with it, quarrels that were no longer settled in each other's arms. What Emmy and Bart shared was ultimately no more than the umpteenth love that came down to having to convince the other person that they were the one more beset by madness, the one less in tune with reality. In the end Bart fled to a beardless hepatologist called Patsy.

Emmy remained alone and firmly resolved to look at love from a distance in future. For women that was generally more difficult, she realized, biologically speaking but even more on a semantic level: a man is restless, a woman hysterical. At work she frequently stopped to examine the intriguing portrait of a bald man mounted on the wall in the corridor next to the secretarial offices. Ignaz Semmelweis was his name, according to the caption. Emmy never looked up who he was—she assumed he had something to do with founding the hospital—but because of the portrait she often thought about baldness in men. How baldness is worse in women. How for a man it's no catastrophe if he lacks a beard.

Yet she'd looked into the eyes of enough flawed men to know that despair and impotence were sexless, just like short-sightedness and malice, and Emmy did not wish to become involved with gender-bound misanthropy. The more couples she observed, the more relieved she felt at being spared their exhausting fulfilments in life. You could see it in their faces. Everyone had insulted everyone else again. At home silences or tears would fall, and there were rifts, with an eye to something better, until there was no avoiding the realization that it only ever seems that way.

Emmy Debeuckelaer raced through her life, past adults with dirty nappies, vagrants with psychoses, couples with problems, strangers with stares and recurring extras who liked her but didn't know her. Sometimes she would turn abruptly to people and ask what they were looking at. One time a woman answered: 'I was looking at your dress, it's lovely,' and it cost Emmy quite some effort not to believe her. And every night again: the axe, the screams, the perforated intestines, the taste of human flesh, the relief.

God took all the time in the world to put her patience to the test. She was approaching forty, Emmy was. Her beard was already showing its first grey hairs. The guilt had still not been atoned.

There were days when she doubted whether one lifetime would be enough to set right all Richard's wrongdoing, especially since she enjoyed it so much in her sleep. There were days when the beard seemed more like bad luck after all, days when she no longer believed in recompense, even though she had nothing else to go on, days too when she believed that all goodness begins and ends with yourself, which needn't necessarily be a problem. There were ominous days when she thought: from now on everything is full of flies.

Emmy started to see people who wronged her as ever-shrinking sculptures on the palm of her hand. When she closed and opened it again, they were gone. She learned how to look at people, saw that they could continually and permanently damage themselves by their efforts to change course. She'd finally worked out how to describe what was hidden inside them when they looked at her forested chin; they saw their own scars, concealed in the darkest passageways of their soul, the ghosts of their childhood, the traumas woven into their DNA for generations.

There was a morning when Emmy woke from a dream in which Richard had been lying on his back in the grass staring at the clouds and the migrating birds flying past them. She had no idea what his fourteenth-century brain thought about that, perhaps Richard didn't think anything at all, but it was clear he'd been behaving the same way all night, briefly no longer a slayer. It made her feel as if she'd lost something essential and immediately forgotten what. It felt good.

There are people who laugh till they cry. With Emmy Debeuckelaer it was the other way round. In the deepest pit of her sorrow she suddenly felt immensely happy. What a morning! It was a morning on which she was the only glittering grain in the awe-inspiring mountain of variation that nature had managed to bring forth, not a type that would set the tone for future generations but a sublime one-off. A gift is also an abnormality, went the cry of jubilation in Emmy's chest, and she even turned it around: an abnormality is also a gift. She felt a true and sovereign aristocrat, that morning, and for a handful of mornings after, scattered untidily across a life that advanced just as quickly as anyone else's. As for the beard, that remained.

Rigor Mortis

They'd laughed about him while driving to his house. It wasn't the first time he'd told her a bit about Daniel, and as on previous occasions it won him her gleeful attention. Especially when he imitated Daniel's plaintive way of talking. In the car she stroked his neck with two fingers and pieced the anecdotes together into the man she was about to meet for the first time, the young guy Bart had got to know when he was still a trainee at the hospital, the patient who wanted his hypochondria to be taken seriously, who had actually shouted: 'I'm a hypochondriac, remember?!' That bozo who wanted to be an actor but never got beyond playing corpses. Him.

'Is he the one with shingles, too?'

Bart couldn't remember any story about shingles, not even imaginary shingles, not even a made-up story.

'I don't think so, no.'

Clearly there must be someone else in her past who told anecdotes about strange friends. Bart felt a stab of jealousy and didn't mind that at all. It meant something, to feel jealous. It'd been a while.

'And why does a doctor become friends with a hypochondriac?'

'Shared interests?'

She grinned for a second or two, then asked, genuinely

curious: 'No, really. Why are we going to see him? He sounds terrible, in real life.'

'He's a source of good stories,' said Bart. 'It's his house-warming.'

And Daniel wasn't terrible in real life. Or not terrible, full stop. He hoped Patsy would realize that. He felt certain she would.

The front door was open a crack, so they went in. They stopped in the dark hallway for a chance to absorb the scene in the living room without being noticed.

'It looks like a nativity stall,' Bart muttered.

Daniel was sitting in a chair with a stout woman at his side whom Bart recognized as his older, manic-depressive sister. The empty beer crate between them was playing the part of the crib. Next to them stood three lanky friends with their hands in their pockets. If they'd brought any myrrh, they must have smoked it already.

'Or just a stall,' Patsy whispered. 'It's not too late to go back.'

In one corner of the cupboard-crammed room a poorly tuned radio was playing. Daniel drowned it out.

'Yes, it might seem nice, a house with a garden, but I'm horribly allergic to the poplar. Severely irritated sinuses. Can't sleep for the pain. Constant. Stinging. No, "cutting". A cutting pain, that's what it is. I think I'll be left with permanent damage.'

'Oh, come on, isn't that laying it on a bit thick?' Bart stepped out of the shadow into the living room.

'Bart!'

There. That was one reason. The way Daniel sprang to

his feet and, just before remembering his ailments again, stretched out his arms towards Bart, quickly, like a child greeting a favourite uncle. Patsy must have missed it. She was inspecting the ceiling and the dusty floor across which she was only now shuffling into the room.

'This is Patsy, Daniel. Daniel, Patsy.'

They shook hands.

'So this is her,' said Daniel, his voice flat.

Patsy frowned mildly in Bart's direction. If Daniel had put it another way, if he'd said he'd heard a lot about her, she would have coyly answered 'likewise' and given Bart a quite different look. Daniel's handshake was less limp than she'd expected, as if he were eager to clinch an important deal.

'Like something to drink?'

'Yes, and give these people something too,' said Bart. The sister and the young men nodded gratefully at him. While Daniel searched for a bottle, one of them helped Bart turn over two sofas that were leaning against the wall on their ends, surrounded by cupboards. When both were standing on the floor in the usual manner, the entire gathering immediately sat on them.

Bart winked at Patsy. She could see how happy he was.

'Showtime!' Daniel called out. His sister took the bottle and glasses from him, so he could hunt for the remote control.

'Did you see me in *City Patrol 2020*?'

Patsy gave him a friendly shake of the head.

'The police series?'

'I haven't seen it,' said Patsy. 'It's not a series I know.'

He turned on the TV and searched through the list of

missed programmes. When he'd found the right episode, he pressed fast forward. The guests attentively followed what was happening on the screen. A policewoman jerkily tapped a policeman on the shoulder. She had a sandwich for him. They both became agitated by it. Agitated robots.

'Press a couple more times. It'll go faster,' said Bart. He giggled.

The policewoman drove furtively past a building. Through the bars of a school gate she looked at a child. She walked along a corridor, in the dark. A weapon on the floor. A man on the floor.

'That was me,' said Daniel. 'Dammit.'

The remote control wasn't working properly. Bart was laughing at full volume now. Daniel thought it was funny as well. A block of flats in the sun. The counter of a pastry shop. The tearful face of a woman. The counter of a pastry shop. A block of flats in the sun. A man on the floor. A weapon on the floor.

'Stop!' shouted Bart.

'Here I am,' Daniel said unassumingly.

He was shown in close-up for about two seconds. Daniel as a corpse, dried blood in his nostrils and at the corners of his mouth, pale-faced, a memory of some superhuman depravity in his bulging eyes. Then the policewoman spoke into her smartphone. 'I have him,' she said. 'He got here before us. Come to the warehouse.' And Daniel lay on the floor behind her like an out-of-focus prop. To round off the scene the camera zoomed in on him one more time.

'Dan the man!' shouted Bart.

'Dead man Dan!' shouted Daniel.

The three skeletal young men and the sister grinned along with them for a moment.

'There's something else,' said Daniel. He stood up. 'Would you mind taking a quick look? It's a kind of skin rash. It started the day before yesterday. I think it's shingles. Come with me to the kitchen, the light's better in there.'

'Shingles?' said Bart. 'Shingles after all. Patsy, did you hear that?'

A weak smile flashed across her face.

'Does your brother often play the corpse?' she asked the sister, after Bart and Daniel had closed the kitchen door behind them. 'I mean, can you earn a living that way?'

The sister shrugged.

Patsy looked at the closed door and felt something she couldn't immediately place, until she realized it was fear.

'He's been in several feature films,' said one of the men. 'He's famous, really.'

Patsy nodded. Perhaps the young man had meant it purely informatively. Perhaps it wasn't a rebuke.

'What do you do?' asked the one sitting next to him.

He hadn't said: what are you doing here? There was probably no need for her to be on her guard.

'I'm a doctor,' said Patsy. 'Like Bart. We're doctors. Bart's a urologist and I'm a liver specialist. We work at the same hospital. But in different departments, of course.'

It was as if she'd been talking for ages, in an inappropriately loud voice. As if she'd given secrets away. What were they up to in that kitchen?

The last dribble of wine stuck stubbornly to the bottom of the glass before finally rolling over the rim onto Patsy's tongue.

39

Bart noticed she was glaring at him when he burst into the living room sniggering. First he pushed Daniel towards her, then he pulled up his shirt a little. His fingers made slight depressions in the pulpy flesh of Daniel's belly, right next to his navel.

Patsy scratched herself at the same spot.

'What do you reckon that is?' asked Bart affectionately. 'I'd say they were mosquito bites.'

'It's too dark in here,' she said, before even looking.

'They're in a neat row,' Daniel observed. 'Pretty intense for a simple mosquito.'

Bart rolled his eyes. For Patsy's benefit. Was she supposed to smile? What did he expect?

'You want to watch the scene?' Without waiting for an answer, Daniel pulled a DVD out of its case. It seemed he'd put it ready.

'Is that the rigor mortis?' How could Bart ask in such a neutral tone?

'He's really terrific in that,' the sister whispered.

After fifteen minutes, Daniel found the right fragment of a costume drama, the kind that Bart called 'garden viewing'. Daniel played a genteel coachman who was shot with an old-fashioned handgun. He stared open-mouthed at the expanding patch of blood amid the frills of his shirt and then sank sideways to the ground.

Patsy's eyes moved back and forth between the screen and the breathless viewers.

Bart massaged her calf.

'That doesn't make sense!' She'd restrained herself as long as she could.

The thin men and the sister stared at her, plainly insulted. But she was angrier. She pointed at Daniel, then at the screen.

'Your character is shot and then immediately starts to go stiff. That's not what happens! Rigor mortis doesn't set in until two hours after you die, and six hours later the body goes limp again. I'm a doctor. My mother …'

They didn't need to know that. First her mother's eyelids, then from her cheeks to her neck, then the rest, in a wave. She needed to calm down. Bart stroked her knee. Daniel poured more wine into her glass. When she put it to her lips she felt a vague pain starting up in her stomach.

After the rigor mortis scene came three more clips in which Daniel breathed his last. In one he swerved a car into the path of an oncoming vehicle, in another he tried in vain to avoid a collision, and in the third his lifeless body was found on a beach.

After a mischievous 'That's all, folks' and brief applause from the audience, Daniel turned off the television.

Patsy had clapped along with them, listlessly. A ball of lava seemed to have settled into her stomach. 'I don't feel well,' she said to Bart. Had he heard her?

Daniel liked to talk about his hypochondria. He'd declined treatment because he had his own theories about its underlying causes.

'I remember once getting a nasty burn as a child and being surprised that there was an ointment for it. The existence of both injury and treatment struck me as an error that didn't fit in the ideal world I longed for. My hypochondria is a way of dealing with that. A reaction.'

Everyone nodded.

'I don't understand,' said Patsy.

'For a long time I struggled with a similar thought,' said Bart. 'Why do frogs exist? Okay, they eat insects. But why do insects exist? Why all the carry-on? Who knows, maybe that's why I became a doctor.'

'What?' She'd never heard him say anything so obtuse.

Something was wrong with her breathing, with the air. If her stomach wasn't hurting so much, she'd think she was dreaming. She tried to squash the fireball flat with her fists. It must have something to do with the wine. Poison. The wine must be poisoned. Daniel was trying to poison her. Perhaps she ought to empty the glass into her handbag so she could have the wine analysed in a laboratory, then she'd have proof. No. She put the half-empty glass on the floor and carefully pushed it away with her foot. When she looked up again, her eyes caught the sister's, those grey eyes like narrow slits in a broad face. The light shining out of them was clear and cold.

Madness floated like a swarm of fireflies through the dimly lit living room, buzzed against the high ceilings of the musty house and circled around Patsy's head. It was infectious. Tangible.

She stood up.

'I don't feel well.'

'What did you say, my love?'

Bart walked up behind her.

'Open it!' Patsy shouted.

He fumbled in his trouser pockets for the car keys and opened the door from a distance. She settled herself behind the wheel, even though Bart had been driving.

'Patsy, what's wrong?'

She mustn't say anything about poison. 'I've got such a stomach ache. I want to go home.'

Disappointment crept over him, he still didn't exactly know why.

'Of course, my sweet. Just come and say goodbye to Daniel. Come on. So strange that you suddenly ran off.'

She tried to sound unmoved. 'I'm strange?'

'It's not surprising if you don't feel entirely comfortable, but try getting to know him better. Come back inside with me for a moment.'

'My stomach really hurts! I think it's the wine.'

'Okay,' said Bart. He didn't believe her and was making no effort to hide it.

'Who are those people, Bart? What are they to you? Do you want to help him? Daniel? Is that it? Aren't your patients enough for you?'

'That's not it,' said Bart. No, that wasn't it.

'What were you doing in the kitchen?'

'What do you mean?'

'Is there something between the two of you?'

He shook his head, as if overcome by a sudden dreaminess. He wondered who this woman could be. This Patsy. Four months ago she'd stayed the night with him for the first time. At breakfast she drew a face on his egg and folded a paper hat for it. She was beautiful, sweet, sensible and funny. But that wasn't all.

'It really does hurt!'

He could see what she must have been like as a child,

when she wanted something she couldn't get, got something she didn't want. The face on the egg had looked sad, almost conflicted. He could give her a hug, let her start the car. 'Come with me for a moment,' he said, his fist already on the door handle.

'No! Stay here!' Bart would never re-emerge. Daniel would never let him go. She'd be left waiting here while her hair turned grey and her nails grew in circles.

'I'm going to get my coat. I'll be right back.'

'You weren't wearing a coat!' she shouted after him. The car door shut off her voice with a bang.

By the time Bart walked back into the living room, everyone had gathered around Daniel and his cello. That was another reason: the cello. The way he meekly bent his head as he played, the long glide of the bow, the stiff finger of a trembling hand pressing a string. The piece evoked a deep blue sea under a coral-coloured sky, the smell of food from small kitchens in whitewashed houses, children playing in the middle of a crowded square, surrounded by voices and evening, and all of it breathing a kind of regret.

'I call it "The Apocalypso",' said Daniel after the silence and the applause.

'It was beautiful.' Bart swallowed. 'Patsy ought to have heard that. She's in the car, says she doesn't feel well, wants to go home.'

'Have some patience with her,' said Daniel. 'Give her a chance.'

Biographer

The boys wouldn't be there at all if he hadn't met Tatiana. But there they were, and when they stayed with him Alex had to control himself or he'd be forever sniffing at their heads, gently pinching their limbs, stroking their backs. The twins patiently endured all his fondling, as if listening to his hands. Sometimes they climbed unexpectedly into his lap or put their arms round his neck. They acknowledged him. Yet he didn't want to be overly affectionate for fear that, converted into the language of five-year-olds, it might lead to dangerous misunderstandings on the part of their mother, friends' parents, primary school teachers, all those people in whom he felt he aroused distrust. He wanted to see his children more often. One weekend a fortnight wasn't enough.

So he usually stuck to looking and listening. Like now. He'd pulled up a chair next to their play mat. Elbows on his knees, he was observing their game, something with a plastic car that you had to wind up and then assemble inside a certain time; slowness was punished with parts springing out in all directions. They'd brought the toy from their mother's place, 'from home' as they put it. The building blocks and colouring books he'd gathered in seemed to hold little appeal.

'Daddy?'

That was Roman, looking up at him. Often the boy didn't swallow properly and as usual he seemed unaware of the saliva dripping from his open mouth as he sat intently playing. Andreas showed more signs of intelligence. That had been obvious to Alex even during their first few months and now that they were five, other people had started to notice as well. Dizygotic twins. Alex sometimes caught himself wondering how such a thing could happen, how a damaged spermatozoid could have reached its target as quickly as its flawless rival. Or did the fault lie with one of Tatiana's eggs? There were so many important things you couldn't find out, so many answers that led you further away from the essence.

'Daddy?'

'Yes, Roman?'

'I think you're sweet.'

The essence.

'I think you're sweet too, kiddo.'

So sweet I could eat you up, he thought, but he kept that to himself, it was one of those sayings that might have unpleasant consequences—nightmares, reprimands, denunciations.

'What was it you said you do?' asked Andreas, probably because of a need to cut through the syrupy air hanging between his father and brother.

'I'm a bi-o-grapher. A biographer writes books about people's lives.'

He didn't want to think beyond the sound and definition of the word.

'Why?' asked Andreas, verging on insolence.

Alex sighed. 'Because.'

'Because isn't an answer,' said Andreas.

Why? Because for a long time he'd been convinced he had a nose for unique people, for lives he was duty-bound to preserve for future generations, even if future generations were already wondering why.

'Want something more to drink?' Before the boys could answer, Alex stood up. He fetched two packs of apple juice from the fridge and handed them out.

Sometimes he thought he'd chosen biographies mainly because he wanted to write but couldn't see the point of invented characters when reality was a treasure trove of unwritten life stories, or because stories previously told needed correcting. At other times he saw the whole thing differently; then it came down to the fact that he wasn't any good at thinking up subjects.

'Daddy?'

'Hold your drink right up to your lips, Roman, you're spilling it.'

Roman looked at the wet patches on his clothes.

'What were you going to say?'

'Will you write about us as well?'

'No, not you.'

The question had surprised him and the indignation that greeted his answer was completely unexpected.

'We've got lives too, haven't we?' said Andreas.

'I had no idea you wanted me to. Maybe I will after all,' he said simply. 'When you're big.'

It would be wrong to say anything about what they'd need to achieve before there was a chance their biographies might be written. He didn't want to set standards too high, although he wondered whether it was really true that he wished them happiness instead of success, moderation rather than impressive antics—whether he could see happiness and success as two separate things. If he did describe their childhoods, he would make Roman smarter and Andreas sweeter, or exaggerate the contrast a bit for dramatic reasons.

'Biographers often write about people who're dead.'

He cursed himself when he saw their faces. He'd invited the idea of death, the idea of their death, to sit down on the play mat between them. Every time he tried to explain something he managed to alarm the boys. Who could say how much his ham-fistedness had already marred the first chapter of their biography, despite all his efforts to ensure they avoided the childhood traumas he wrote about.

'But,' said Andreas. Alex could already sense it was going to be another tiresome question. 'If the people are dead, how do you know what you've written is right?'

'What do you mean?' asked Alex. He knew what his son meant. The question filled him with admiration and annoyance.

'They can't read the book and say it's right, can they.'

'You can't ever be completely certain anyhow,' he said. 'The most important thing is that it's a good story. Sometimes people don't know themselves what's right. Even people who're still alive, I mean.'

'They must do. Surely.' Andreas looked genuinely interested. Roman was gathering up exploded car parts.

'I prefer writing about dead people.' Alex felt awkward.

'Why?' This child might grow up to be a hard-boiled detective, famous for his persistent interrogation techniques and his dogged way of staring at you. You're five, for God's sake, Alex wanted to shout.

'Because,' he said.

The disdain with which Andreas turned his attention back to his toys would no doubt hang over him all weekend.

After he'd put the children to bed, he sat in front of the television for a long time before it dawned on him what he was watching. This must be *La Vache et le prisonnier*, in which Fernandel plays a French prisoner of war who escapes from the Germans during the Second World War, on foot, with a cow on a rope and a milk pail in his hand, a cover so simple he manages to sustain it for an entire odyssey. During the scene where he's forced to leave the cow behind so he can board a train bound for France as a stowaway, Alex wondered what was wrong with him; he didn't even like animals. The ending, when Fernandel's character hides in a train in a French railway station that takes him back into Germany, Alex had seen coming. It was probably a metaphor for the impossibility of escaping your fate, the impossibility of flight, the kind of tragicomic shrug he really couldn't stand. He saw himself as someone who confronted setbacks and horrors head-on, who always felt he was capable of improvement, and because of that belief managed to raise himself above the average.

In bed, the sense of something he couldn't quite bring to mind kept him awake. It had to do with the questions his son had asked and with the film he'd just seen. It was an invisible presence pacing back and forth around his bed, settling down over him like a patch of fog. In the distance a feeble

49

glimmer of light appeared. Favarque, thought Alex.

Almost a year ago he'd consigned the biography of Dominique Favarque to a drawer, after 180 pages of typing and months of intensive research. In abandoning the project he'd woken up to the fact that his nose for lives worth writing about had misled him this time, that his predictions were wrong. Having followed the author closely, he'd become convinced Favarque would peak in the next three years, that a magnum opus was in prospect, several more important prizes, maybe even a nomination for the Nobel. His biography would be greeted with astonishment because several years earlier Favarque had stopped talking to the press and appearing at literary events. The mystery had made the media and the public hungry, but then came the dyke breach in Favarque's head last year, on a balcony with a sea view. Blood had swamped all memories. The motor system that writing requires was still intact, the doctors said, but the meaning behind the words, or at the very least the need to read them and write them down, was completely gone. Dominique Favarque, protected from the outside world by a live-in nurse, had not put a single word to paper since. After that day Alex needed to visit the author only once, needed to encounter that confused glance only once to determine that this life without apotheosis was not worth conserving. He had his reputation to think of. His previous work, a biography of Ignaz Semmelweis, the nineteenth-century discoverer of bacteria, had sold poorly but been well received. Financial concerns must not be allowed to affect the quality of his work—even though after laying aside the Favarque project he hadn't managed to start a new book; even though child maintenance and the rent left him barely enough for a life of extreme frugality. If his subject disappointed him, then the book would too. That conviction meant he had to set limits. In future he must concern himself with dead celebrities only.

For now it remained a secret that he was the only person to have managed to wrest any interviews from Favarque in the years between the withdrawal from the world and the stroke. Since the book would never be finished, he was considering adapting them into newspaper articles and selling them to the highest bidder. His failure to do so as yet meant he still hadn't completely let go of the biography, he realized with embarrassment. The fact that after all these months he was leafing through the manuscript again, long after midnight, was another indication. He was looking for something that didn't add up, a truth concealed behind the vague foreboding that was taxing his nerves.

The sleepless night made him none the wiser. In fact by the time it got light his thoughts had turned from Dominique Favarque to his Jaguar. It had cost Alex too much time— and in the end too much money—to get hold of all the parts for the E-type. When the vintage car was at last patched up, driving it didn't bring him the gratification he'd expected. As he listened to his sons clatter down the stairs, he decided to acknowledge defeat and sell the Jaguar—with hurt pride and perhaps at a loss, but the proceeds would give him a chance to haul himself back onto dry land professionally. He must take another trip with the boys today; they loved the car in the way that he'd wanted to. He wouldn't tell them the Jag might not be there a fortnight from now. Who could say how long it might take to find a buyer?

In the bath Roman mimicked a sea lion. It was a convincing imitation that made his brother and his father laugh loudly. Andreas tried to copy him but stopped when he realized Roman was far better at it. Remarkable, Alex thought. Dramatic talent—was that possible? And again he was struck by the feeling that had come over him during the night, of being on the verge of knowing. Fernandel, Favarque—he'd almost got it when he tugged himself back abruptly as an all-too-enthusiastic Roman the sea lion tried to slide off the edge of the bath onto the tiled floor. He caught him in a towel.

At the wheel, on the way to the park, he again tried to trace the connection he'd so nearly arrived at. He was barely aware of the boys urging him from the back seat to go faster, singing a song they'd made up about a speedy Jaguar.

In the park he felt annoyed when someone came to sit next to him on the bench, a black man who pointed out that their pairs of twins were playing together, something Alex could easily have deduced from the scene at the climbing frame. He wanted to think, alone. To his displeasure the man seemed to feel a need to tell his life story, speaking too softly, in French.

'I haven't lived in Mali for fifteen years,' he said. 'I was visiting my family when I met my wife. We rang each other a lot and the next time I flew there she fell pregnant. We got married. I worked seventy hours a week, never went out, rented a nice house and bought a car, made sure everything was ready for a family. When I went to fetch her and the babies at the airport, I felt rich and strong. She could be so funny, my wife, so quick-witted. We lived together for three years, had differences of opinion, never arguments, took it in turns to cook, set records on the fitness machine we'd bought, waved to the children together on their first day at school.'

'Hm,' Alex growled. He didn't want to hear this story. It made him think of Tatiana, the good part of their time together, before she'd had enough of what she called his extremism.

'And then, that very evening, after the first school day— we're watching television, I'm eating chips—she says, "You surely don't think I came to Belgium for you?" I laugh, because she liked jokes, my wife, she was full of wisecracks. But still, the way she's looking at me. She shows me her suitcase and leaves a couple of hours later, without a backward glance, without children. I'm not allowed to know where she lives. Her lawyer thinks I hit her.'

'Jesus,' said Alex. It was only now that he looked the African full in his sorrowful face. Those drooping eyelids. This had nothing to do with Tatiana. Yet the man's story seemed to call up another analogy, which came crawling out of the sandpit. A solution to the puzzle that had been keeping him awake rushed across the grass towards him and was now near the legs of the bench, ready to climb into his lap.

'And what I keep asking myself,' the man went on, 'is whether all that time, right from the beginning ...' He looked up at Alex in anguish. 'What do you think?'

'She was play-acting,' said Alex.

On the highway to the sea the boys sang an atonal song with the lyrics 'Our Jaguar is faster than a panther'. Alex whistled cheerfully over it. He wouldn't sell the car.

Favarque, he thought. Was it possible? Could the author's

confusion at their last meeting have been mere play-acting? He tried to recall the moment he was shown out—'take care,' he'd stammered—and he imagined the rigid muscles around Favarque's eyes relaxing behind the closed door. A smile, even a brief grin, and then, who knows, back to the desk, to the new book. Was it a magnum opus in the making? Would it be published under a pseudonym? Was it already out? Alex ran through the most eulogized debuts of the past year. No, the book couldn't have been published yet.

The longer he thought about it, the more convinced he became of the deception. Fantastic, he thought, that the author had got away with feigning memory loss. At the same time it was as simple as a cow on a rope. In fact it was obvious. To shake off not just the media and literary organizers but the pushy biographer, Favarque had thought up a great disappearing act. It explained why Alex had been unable to find any witnesses to the stroke. Press releases often went unverified. In a delicate matter like this, who would dare to cast doubt on the author's integrity?

Dominique Favarque: a brilliant cheat, convincing as a central character. Bull's eye. Right choice—that above all.

'Why are you laughing, Dad?'

'Because I'm happy, Roman.'

He parked the car next to the dyke and let Roman and Andreas choose a bucket and two spades in a shop. On the beach adults were walking around in thicker coats than his children's, leaning forwards into the wind.

'You go and sit there,' he said. 'I'm staying here.' He pointed to a spot under the sea wall.

'Why aren't you coming with us?' asked Andreas.

'You can manage perfectly well on your own.'

His rear end was getting cold and numb from the blue-stone he was sitting on. Apart from that it was a great spot: he had a clear view of the front of the house.

'The sand's no good here,' said Andreas.

'Then you need to dig deeper,' said Alex.

'We're not digging, we're making a castle!'

He took no further notice, determined not to miss a single movement at the window.

'Daddy?'

Could he perhaps ring the doorbell? A spontaneous visit with the children, out of concern. Maybe quickly buy a cake? The nurse would refuse to let him in; she'd done that before.

'Daddy?'

The front door. He must concentrate on that.

'Daddy?'

'Yes, Roman. What now?'

'It's raining.'

He was about to say it was only a few drops when the clouds began ditching their contents over them at full intensity.

'Come up to the car, quick.'

The children were soaked by the time they crawled onto the back seat with their bucket and spades. Alex was just about to get into the driver's seat when the front door opened and an umbrella was thrust out. He felt his heartbeat quicken. Favarque? No, it must be the nurse, strange person that she was. You're the milk pail, he thought. And the memory loss is the cow.

'Come on Dad! You're getting wet!'

This would be his chance to go into the house and catch the author alone, at the computer, perhaps, or stretched out on the chaise longue, poetry collection in hand. In his rearview mirror he noticed the boys' lips had gone blue. Just one more moment.

'I want to go home,' said Andreas. 'I want to go home!'

'Just one more moment.'

He started the engine then after all, because Tatiana rang, because she asked what he was doing still there at the seaside, whether he thought their agreements didn't matter and whether that was Andreas she could hear crying in the background. But he'd be back, he'd lurk in wait for months if he had to, until he spotted an inconsistency in the performance, until he caught Favarque out. After that he would finish the book, with a devastating disclosure in the final chapter, the justification for his story, for a life.

Dog Without a Name

Samba stretches out on the white leather sofa, making the dog nestle up to her all over again. She strokes him and squints at the bright sun spearing in through the skylights. With one bare foot she taps the back of the laptop screen. Steve ignores the foot, so she uses it to push his screen slowly downwards. He enfolds the limb in his hand.

'Don't be naughty,' he says, his eyes still on something that's making him grin. Prepared for an unavoidable conversation, he takes an earpiece out of his ear.

'Push my feet back.' She tries to make her command sound endearing.

'There's nothing wrong with your feet,' he says absently.

'Look, then!'

Together they look at the feet, which at rest are almost fully stretched out, the toes with yellow-painted nails almost touching the sofa, the white soles invisible.

'You're doing that on purpose.'

'No I'm not. High heels. That's what causes it. My calf muscles have shrunk.'

'You've got the longest calves I've ever seen,' he says, pushing her toes upwards until foot and lower leg form a right angle. 'My black hyena.' He turns his attention back to the screen.

'Hyena?' she asks. Steve is thirteen years older, but less clever. He means gazelle.

'Or, what's it called?' he says. 'Okapi?'

Receiving no answer, he reinserts the earpiece. In weather like this his skin turns rosy, his blond eyebrows prominent against it.

The large coffee table is an oblong of dirt at the heart of the spotless room. The greasy stains on the pizza boxes invite flies, but the fitted insect screens are doing their job. Next to the full ashtray lies a Hello Kitty mirror showing the trail of the greedy, saliva-dipped finger that snaffled up the last bits of coke. Samba was given the mirror when she was six, by a boy in her street who was later run over and killed. Steve doesn't know that.

She puts her feet on the white-stained parquet. Bending forward, she grabs her ankles to stretch her calves. She becomes aware of Steve intrusively feeling her shorts, touching her bottom. When she delivers a sharp slap she realizes it's actually a schnauzer snout she's dealing with.

'Sorry,' she says to the startled dog. She briefly strokes his head.

Steve is still grinning at the screen. He hasn't noticed a thing.

She empties the ashtray into pizza packaging, piles up the boxes and takes them to the kitchen. When she gets back she looks over Steve's shoulder at a clip from a documentary on YouTube. Several women in light-blue boiler suits line up in a row. Two Mexican women are arguing and one is restrained by a guard.

'Fat arses,' Steve grins.

She doesn't want to ask him why he's watching this. She once heard a guest on a talk show say you must never ask about things you don't want to know. It was a casual remark, and the guest may never have given it any great weight, but since then Samba has held her tongue several times a day on the basis of that advice.

When she goes to sit next to Steve, he rotates the screen so that she can watch as well. He also gives her an earpiece.

'I'm looking for a bit of film I can't seem to find, but you have to see this,' he says.

Short blond hairs grow on the finger he's moving across the touchpad.

'Here,' he says.

The guard opens a room, a bathroom or kitchen. The tiled floor and walls are smeared with blood. In the rust-coloured stains are the outlines of hands and feet. Samba thinks she can make out the prints of a pair of knees in one corner.

'Spunky ladies,' coos Steve enthusiastically. 'Watch now.'

The camera glides across a number of confiscated weapons. The sock with the solid object inside and the razor blade with a toothbrush handle melted around it seem to be Steve's particular favourites. Next the film zooms in on photos of scars, mainly on black skin.

Samba's aversion to scars is not a matter of aesthetics. What horrifies her is that they make visible the memory of pain. Bodies are silent about past kisses and touches. At most a little ill-defined goose-flesh appears and disappears when a snatch of departed tenderness crosses the path of thought. All our youth will be forgotten by our skin, muscles and bones. The only tangible souvenirs the body retains are those conferred on it by knives, stones, nails, teeth, and glass.

'Why are you laughing?' she almost asks. But because she doesn't want to know, she says instead: 'Like some chorizo? There's still some chorizo. It needs eating up.'

Steve doesn't want anything. Samba packs the chorizo into a sandwich. After two bites she feeds it to the dog. Even while swallowing, the animal reads her thoughts—that he still needs a walk and that Steve probably won't want to take him out.

Samba comes up to him with the leash. She puts on a pair of trainers. 'I'm going for a walk,' she says.

She likes the hottest days: petrol smell caught between the gasping house fronts, impassive shadows under swollen tree crowns, the endless ringing of ice cream vans, timber settling with a cracking sound. Days like this are made for her, for her skin, which gets warmer and more relaxed with every step, possibly remembering something of a native country that's alien to her.

She manages in the nick of time to pull the dog away from the wheels of a passing car. Through the open sunroof an unintelligible curse flies in her direction.

She takes the animal by the collar and turns its head towards her. Not wanting to be someone who talks to a dog, she simply looks sternly into his round eyes. She's never been able to make this schnauzer out. She usually has no idea why he's wagging his tail, barking or growling. He sometimes eats a lot, sometimes little, his behaviour alternating between devotion and indifference. She understands why Steve couldn't think of a name for him. When she tries to come up with one herself there's nothing that fits. Oddly enough, he seems to respond when someone calls out the name of his mistress.

Samba. There needed to be a link with Africa, her adoptive parents felt. Samba Devleesschouwer. They say they were unaware in those days of the Latin American style of music and dance, and of what she discovered later for herself, that Samba is a West African man's name. Good people, her adoptive parents. She shouldn't have thrown their furniture, ought to visit them more. But when you choose a name for a person you're intending to call your child, surely it's not too much of an effort to check what it means. And if you bring someone into this world, then surely it's your natural duty to find a way to care for them. It seems obvious that her real mother hasn't missed her for a second, no matter how many times her Belgian father says there are no grounds for thinking that. It's her certainty, for as long as she can remember: not being missed.

Samba's no name for a schnauzer anyhow.

When a truck passes, the dog jumps at the wheels again. It's as if he's had enough of life, summer or not.

To head off further attempts, Samba pulls the dog into the park. A young father on a patchwork rug on the grass looks at her shorts with an idiotic smile and the eyes of a fox, while gently pressing a rattle to the ear of his unquestionably self-begotten baby. The child, undergoing the offensive with surprise, stops reaching out and topples over.

From a park bench, Samba watches the people. Their existence disturbs her intensely. How they try to reassure themselves. The toasts, the sustained friendships, the melted cheeses in their picnic baskets. She doesn't believe them, doesn't believe that the ugliest woman in the park can have confidence in her hairstyle, the airhead in his talents, the adolescents in their youth. She thinks she knows their secrets: the crying bouts on the toilet, the binoculars, the dreams of adultery, the lock-up garage, who said of whom that they stink. There was a time when she wanted to be part of this herd. She wonders whether it's good if such a desire dies. Looking at these people now she can even understand why she stays with Steve: there's no elsewhere that would be any better.

The dog strangles itself with the leash. Maybe it wants to walk. Maybe it wants to die. Samba stands up. Her feet need to march, jump, kick.

She's just out of the park when someone sends her a text. The sender's number is unknown to her.

'I love you,' it says.

She resolves not to give her number to people who ask for it in future, not even after a sixth glass of wine.

'I'm pregnant,' she writes back. The unknown person must at least be made to think her life has taken a drastic turn.

She's just about to put the phone away when an answer comes in. 'Not true,' it says, followed by an emoticon whose mood escapes her.

When she throws the phone into a bush, the dog looks at her as if he's no time for childish behaviour. Samba can see that he has a point. She fishes the phone out of the dead leaves, removes the battery and puts it in her right hip pocket, the empty phone in her left. She mustn't let herself be delayed by anything else now.

'Hello, sister,' says a fat black man. Eating a nectarine, he leers at her.

'I don't have any brothers,' says Samba. She doesn't notice the man whistle through his teeth disapprovingly as she walks off.

At a bakery she buys two croissants, one for herself and one for the dog. She wants to get out of town, to walk in the woods, and she takes unknown streets in the hope they'll become dirt tracks, looking for ways into hidden fields behind the rows of houses. But every gravel path turns out to be a driveway, every lane strands her in a modern housing estate. The houses seem herded together by the traffic encircling the suburb. Heavy, hot air rolls over low roofs, then lies stretched out on the streets. Although the schnauzer tends to trip over his own tongue, he patters along at a steady pace.

The sweating croissants have turned the paper bag transparent. Samba leans against a letter box shaped like a house, a miniature version of the one to which it belongs. She breaks a croissant in half and gives half to the dog. He doesn't even snuffle at it but turns his head and stares at the cartwheel bricked into the low front-garden wall.

'*Est-ce que je peux vous aider?*' asks a balding man in his forties with a Flemish accent. Samba is surprised she didn't hear him coming. He's wearing flip-flops and Bermuda shorts made of parachute fabric; he surely must have made some noise as he walked towards her from the house. In the window she can see the outline of a woman, chin in the air and hands in the dishwasher, awaiting her husband's successes.

'*Tu me comprends?*' asks the man, because she's been too

slow to answer. Although she is now sizing him up disparagingly, he goes on firing questions at her. '*Madame …*' he says, articulating as if to a deaf-and-dumb elderly lady, '*Qu'est-ce que tu fais ici?*' And then: 'You speak English? How did you come here?'

It occurs to her to answer in broken English that she crossed the ocean in a leaky, overloaded boat. That she survived by eating dead passengers. That she's been addicted to human flesh ever since. But it's so hot today, and her feet are itching to feel the street.

So instead she says stiffly, 'I'm eating a croissant, sir.'

'And does that have to happen here?' he asks.

She studies his small frame. From the fluctuations of his T-shirt she can tell he's breathing rapidly, that he's afraid. On the inside of his forearm is a tattoo of a Chinese character that she hopes means something other than what he thinks: 'fear' instead of 'strength', 'snot' rather than 'hero'.

Then she hears the swelling growl. For a moment she thinks it's her own anger, raging inside her ribs and encircling her head like a tingling crown. When she sees a flash of white teeth she realizes it's coming from the schnauzer. He's defending her, or at least he shares her opinion.

The growling fascinates Samba. The dog has never done this before. She kneels down beside him and feels a gurgle in his warm flank. When she puts her ear to his fur, he goes quiet.

'Come on, take that dangerous creature with you and move it!' the man shouts. The indistinct woman in the window forgets about doing the dishes and thrusts her chin slightly higher into the air.

Samba walks away. She hasn't felt any anger since the dog growled. Before turning into another street, she looks round one more time at the man. He's bending down over the half-croissant she left in the grass, which he picks up with his handkerchief and carries away before him as if it's an amputated finger. The woman opens the door to let him in.

Samba walks aimlessly for several miles, until she unexpectedly spots a river amid lush vegetation. She's aware of the muscles in her lower legs and the space in her head, ready for a road worth following. The river cuts across a patchwork of green, brown, and yellow fields. She uncouples the leash. The dog immediately runs off ahead.

'Wait!' she calls after him. The laugh in her voice startles her.

He alters neither direction nor speed. For half an hour, an hour, an hour and a half she follows his trail over the fields. Now and then they cross an unsealed road; at one point two horses walk with them for a while. Samba must find a way of running without ever stopping. Every time she thinks she's lost the dog, only for him to turn up again, she gets the impression he's waiting for her. Her T-shirt is soaked with salty sweat, the leather of the leash smells of her hand, her hand of the leather; dandelion fluff sticks to her forehead and in her hair. The sky becomes whiter, harder, heavier. Let it rain, she thinks, on me and that dog.

Before seeing the highway she can hear it, and when she sees it she knows where she is. She recognizes the bridge, the exit that Steve takes when they're driving to his apartment. She can't fathom how that's possible. She thought she was running in a straight line. It must have been a huge circle.

Panting, she slows down.

'Wait!' she shouts, out of breath. And when that has no effect: 'Samba!'

The dog looks round, seems to hesitate and walks on, past a field of flax, then a strip of tall grass where, with the last of her strength, she catches up, drops on top of him, and wrestles to put on the leash. His tongue is hanging out of his mouth, his breath blows hot against her shoulder, the fur he loses sticks to her sweat. Then she knows what she needs: someone who'll take her out in the evening, point to the sky and say, 'That's Venus, the brightest of all the planets, and tomorrow Saturn will be visible briefly, don't forget.'

The dog has turned its wild eyes to the highway again. Samba can't hold him back. She wraps the leash around her arm and allows herself to be pulled along, flying and stumbling behind him faster than her feet can carry her. Together then, she thinks.

But as she approaches the hard shoulder, which borders the fields, something bends her to its will so that she frees her arm from the leash, knowing he'll slip loose.

Without the slightest hesitation the dog plunges into the braking, skidding traffic. Twice there's a dull thud. Once she sees him perform a shaky somersault. When a honking delivery van hits the lifeless animal, making it seem as if the dog is back on his feet for a moment, she turns away.

Now she ought to scream. She is lost, exalted, she's jealous of the dog. But she just silently looks at the swaying crowns of the trees as they move with increasing vehemence in a rising, rapidly strengthening blast of wind. Behind her the cars race past like before.

'Miss?' says a soft voice.

Two policemen are looking attentively at her. She tries to run away from them. Her feet are heavy and unstable, as if big sacks of water have been tied around them. She almost falls. One of the men grabs her by the shoulder. Samba sweeps her arm in the direction of the highway. The policemen exchange glances.

'I do understand, you know,' says the one with the quiet voice. 'I have a dog too.'

'You all right?' the other asks.

The policemen wait in the car for Samba to open the front door. When she waves at them, smiling, they nod politely. After a few minutes they come and stand next to her.

'Can't get in?'

'No, it's fine, it's fine,' says Samba. She transfers the bunch of keys from one hand to the other and back. 'My feet weigh rather a lot at the moment, that's all.'

Again she notices them exchange glances.

'It's going to rain,' the quiet one says.

'Yes,' she says.

'May I?' He points to the bunch of keys.

She puts them in his hand and hooks her arm around his. Together they shuffle to the lift, followed by his colleague.

On the top floor, the pinkness drains from Steve's cheeks when he sees the policemen. They explain to him that his dog is dead and his girlfriend in shock.

'Will you be all right?'

Steve, his head full of cold wind, says they will. Samba sidles past him, to the shower.

She can hear him through the spurting water. What was she thinking of? What if the police had followed her into the lounge? He was having a snort!

When she doesn't answer, he tries to think of something comforting to say about the dog. That he lived the life of a prince. 'An easy life,' Steve calls it.

'Look,' he says, when Samba finally comes into the living room. 'I've found that bit of film I wanted to show you.'

A small, round woman sits on a Jamaican prison wall. Armed guards stand on either side, waiting for her to give up. They wait patiently. With a floodlight trained on her, the woman sings an aria about freedom at the top of her lungs. Steve bursts out laughing. After a dignified descent halfway down the ladder, she misses a rung. She lies on the ground until tapped by a foot.

'She gave it a go,' Samba says, not even angry.

A couple of times she sniffs at her hand, concentrating hard. The leather smell of the leash has gone, leaving merely soap. She stretches out on the white leather sofa and looks through the skylight. The sky is still holding back its tears.

Right

No one could say Didier Van Ranst didn't do his best. First he'd asked for the head of department at the employment agency and then, casually, for a local girl. Perturbed by the name Lyuba, he'd repeated his wish, his right, articulating it carefully. It took the head of department a considerable effort to misunderstand him.

So, before you know it, there's one of those round brown things at the door and what do you do then? Didier Van Ranst will tell you what you do then, you let her into your house because you've grown up in a civilized country and you think, with a hope born of desperation, that maybe she'll learn something here.

He has been patient. He never raised his voice to her when she fired incomprehensible questions at him, and if he did catch something—usually something inappropriate: was he unemployed? Was his wife dead?—he simply pretended not to understand those questions either. He ignored her, instead of showing her the door. When she refused to wash the windows with ammonia, even though nothing is more effective against grease, he bought new products for her. Apparently an employment agency can oblige a client to do that. Apparently it's in a contract.

He has seen where she lives. He followed her Fiat Panda

in his own car. He needed to know. And on the outside it was nothing special, that particular block of flats, just as her car would never make you suspect that her husband, or her brother, or her cousin—the fellow she lives with is probably her husband and brother and cousin—has a Mercedes in the garage. He waited to see which light would go on and you might have guessed it was that flat with the geraniums and olive trees on the balcony. Didier Van Ranst knows why trees like that are locked to the fronts of mansions with steel chains, he knows the price of those trees up there on her balcony, high and dry. Another thing he knows is that the head of department at the employment agency won't want to draw any conclusions, won't want to see any connection, and therefore that there's no point in ringing him. Didier Van Ranst puts the receiver down.

She certainly makes it difficult for him to complain, she's not clever but cunning, the house gleams as never before, new dust falls uneasily onto the polished furniture, his houseplants get too much attention—they want to be left in peace.

'Thirsty?' she asks the plants. 'Hungry?' she asks him. He says nothing, restrains himself, waits. She makes blancmange for him. Did he ask her to make blancmange for him? He thought not. He says nothing but thinks a lot.

His brother comes round and he's such a prick, always was. Serge Van Ranst was always allowed, always given, that little bit more. He sets her off laughing. She laughs like a child.

'My brother,' says his brother, 'needs a lot of looking after.' She stops laughing and nods earnestly, sees from his face that she mustn't look at him like that—he wants a flame-thrower—and decides she'll make a joke too.

'You know what is little baby of cardboard box and plastic bag?' she asks. The jolly gypsy. He goes to make coffee. He sees her, reflected in the gleaming kitchen window, produce a paper bag from behind her back. His brother doesn't stop roaring with laughter until Didier orders him to leave.

He rings the employment agency and asks them to send someone else. Apparently he has to have a reason. So much for the customer is king. He knows enough. He makes little towers of coins on the kitchen counter and on the washing machine in the hope they'll be stolen. He hides his watch in the washing so it can be washed and ruined. She puts all the money together on the dining table as if she intends to play shops with it and displays the watch as if in a jeweller's window. She's a challenge. She'll steal something he won't miss for a while, probably has done already. He pulls boxes out of cupboards, things out of boxes, then puts everything back. He must pick the right moment to catch her. At the same time he must be out of the house as much as possible.

He hurries through town, through the puddles, through the ugliness pieced together over the centuries. It's filling the place up. It hangs around shopping centres and drapes itself over benches, it grabs whatever there is to be grabbed, it takes, it took over everything long ago, it can no longer be driven back.

What's he doing here? He's letting his house be taken over too. It's his house, he shouldn't flee, he mustn't leave it defenceless. He returns to demand it back.

He runs up and down the stairs. She's gone—what has she

71

stolen? She's standing at the window in his bedroom, one knee on the windowsill. His bedroom. His window. Does she prostitute herself here? Does she use his bed? How long has this been going on? The clothes she wears, those colours, that roundness. He tells her he doesn't pay her to stand there and she turns and looks at him as if with fondness, but it's scorn.

'A cloud,' she says. 'Look there, a cloud. A swan.' She goes on looking at it with a sweet smile. She's right, he thinks, a swan, with a broken neck.

He pinches her breast hard, twists the skin in his fist. She screams and turns a face up towards him in which surprise wins out over humiliation. 'Are these work clothes?' he asks. 'Is that appropriate?'

She stands there, leaning forward, whimpering in that crook's tongue of hers. When he lets go of her she storms to the door like a clockwork toy, down the stairs and out of the door. Right, thinks Didier Van Ranst. He needs to say it out loud. 'Right.'

Yet he can't shake it off, it follows him day and night: she's going to play a trick on him. She'll distort the story into indecent assault; he knows her sort, her sex, he knows those tricks, the sleight of hand that cost him his job. The head of department at the employment agency—he's listening patiently to her grouching right now, promising to call the police. They won't get anything out of him, he'll show them what keeping your trap shut means, perseverance.

She comes back, tail between her legs, and stands at the door, eyes down, her low neckline replaced by a wide woollen jacket. He lets her slip past him into the hall, motionless on the ropes for a moment. What is this? Self-knowledge? Contrition? A fortuitous absence of consequences? Then he realizes: she's come back with a plan. He has to catch her. It's a matter of life and death now.

Never, he resolves, will he lap up what she serves him. He'll be on his guard. But there's no food any more, only the necessary, only what she's contracted to do, just enough to make complaints seem unreasonable, the witch, the tongue-tied, underhanded bitch.

He abandons the coinage and gets larger and larger bank-notes out of the wall, putting them in places where someone might have forgotten them long ago. She spots every trap. He doesn't give up.

He looks for his digital camera and can't find it—she probably flogged it ages ago to relatives in some primitive settlement with a name consisting entirely of consonants. She'll be expected to do her bit for the household; that brother, cousin, husband of hers will be able to force that much obedience from her, how else did they get the Mercedes?

He finds his camera. She put it in a different place to make him search, to distract his attention.

Then he steps into his cupboard, the wardrobe in his bedroom. It's his wardrobe, he has the right. There he waits.

He waits until she comes into the bedroom holding a vacuum cleaner, its hose round her neck, the way she's carried it before. She looks around, wondering where the booty is. He's ready.

Just pretend, he thinks. Just start in the corners, have a good go under the bed, get down on your knees, bow down, bow to my floor. When she picks up the little box on the bedside table he points the camera at her through the crack. She opens the box, looks in silence at the banknotes—now, he thinks, now I've got you—then shuts it again and runs a duster over it.

She waddles out of the door with the vacuum cleaner. He wonders whether she's coming back. It surely can't be clean enough in here yet. Now here she is again with a bucket and cloth, she seems to want to clean everything, the bedstead, the skirting board—the woman's possessed, is this a case like Macbeth's wife, the eternal hand-washing, wiping clean a bad conscience?

Now it's the turn of the wardrobe. She starts at the bottom, moves on to the side. She bends to rinse and as she straightens up she sees him, through the crack. Their eyes meet. She's startled, takes several steps back. Now he has to react, to hop out of the wardrobe like a hare, but she's ahead of him, throwing her full weight at the door and turning the key. That was it, then, that's what she's driven him to: aiding and abetting her, helping her to catch him. In between his knocks on the inside of the wardrobe he hears her storm down the stairs and slam the front door. She leaves him there in the deepest blackness; it won't be long before the air runs out. She surely won't come back this time, unless it's to strip his house. He'll have to carve the name of his murderess into the wood with his nails. He should have brought a ballpoint. He hates having to die unprepared.

A video message, he thinks. The camera is still in his hand. I'm Didier Van Ranst, cruelly locked in and left for dead in my wardrobe—no, they'll see that, the wardrobe, it mustn't sound comical—by my cleaner Lyuba … what's her surname? Didier Van Ranst turns on the camera and there's the photo of her with the little box on the bedside table, duster in hand. A cleaner, he thinks. To anyone who doesn't know any better, a perfectly ordinary woman.

Shaving Together

Several demonstrators turned angrily towards Josephine. She wasn't planning to drive into the crowd, she'd only tapped the accelerator to rattle them a little. When two burly characters in tight red raincoats strode threateningly in her direction, she tooted a couple of times. The fatter of the two kicked the delivery van. The other pulled him fraternally away and went on staring furiously at Josephine, tapping his head. Around them others followed their example. Scowling. Shouting as they pointed at their foreheads. Raising their fists.

Mass hysteria, Josephine felt. Suddenly everyone was the little man. She had nothing to do with the demonstrators, with the strikers; she had nothing to do with anyone. Although she did see herself as a member of the class these little men and women were rebelling against, so it seemed as if they were rebelling against her.

She'd been tested quite rigorously of late, with that coward of a father-in-law and his sudden decision to retire, just like that, to spite her, leaving her running a company with a book-keeping system only the father-in-law could make head or tail of. Even worse was her disappointing husband, who turned out to drink even during working hours and had been forced to surrender his driving licence for a month.

That meant he couldn't stand in for Brigitta, the person supposedly responsible for transport, who since her boss left had been off work with depression. Josephine was still searching for a way of sacking the autistic layabout, which turned out to be far from straightforward. For the time being she had no other choice but to deliver the catering decorations herself, driving the delivery van. She was determined to save the company and thereby confirm her talent for business, her superiority. If only those demonstrators would get out of the way. She sounded the horn again.

Tearing through a built-up area, she suddenly remembered she needed to call on the Cheries later in the day. Their restaurant was somewhere around here. The Cheries had ordered thirty metres of dummy books and five boxes of candles, subcategory 'Nature'. Months ago now. The quantities had seemed excessive to Josephine even at the time, but for one reason or another—was it the impeccable email? The restaurant's complex logo?—she hadn't asked for a down payment and had sent her husband out that same day with the delivery. It was only later that she noticed the Cheries' website didn't work. There had been no response to her emails and voicemail messages. The bill for 1,717 euros and 88 cents had still not been paid. You couldn't trust anyone.

Perhaps that was the reason Josephine dealt with the manageress of the grocery shop in a somewhat predatory style, even by her own standards. The woman claimed to have ordered a strawberry one metre tall, not 146 centimetres. Her husband and a friend had struggled to lift the colossus out

78

of the van. It blocked the entrance to the shop. The woman flapped the order form to prove herself right.

'Look at it this way, madam,' said Josephine. 'The big one is an eye-catcher, the small one isn't.'

'But you sell the smaller one too, don't you?' the manageress tried.

'Hardly ever. Hence the mistake.' She threw the husband the look she'd been practising ever since her breasts grew.

'Oh well. This strawberry is here now,' said the man. 'And Luc's got to go.'

His friend took stock of her. He was fiddling with something in his coat pockets.

'But Dirk, that thing won't even fit through the door!' the woman wailed.

'Might be better to put it outside anyhow,' said Dirk. 'Next to the entrance. As an eye-catcher.' He looked at Luc, who muttered his agreement, and then at Josephine, with those naughty little wrinkles around her nose. 'Entirely up to you,' they might mean. Or: 'I never wear knickers.'

'Maybe,' said the woman, realizing the decision had already been made.

This strawberry cost 186 euros more than the other.

She still had it in her. Fired by a pugnacious form of narcissism, Josephine arrived at the Cheries' restaurant, which was called Chérie's and had a beautiful exterior.

She rang three times but no one opened the door, even though she was convinced she'd heard music inside, which had stopped abruptly after her first press of the bell. Josephine smelled fear. It fuelled her fighting spirit. The security blinds at the front were down, so she walked to the side wall. With some difficulty she pushed a large rubbish bin out of the way—malodorous but apparently empty. Behind it was an uncurtained window. She immediately recognized what she could see inside: failure, poverty.

Unlaid tables had spread themselves distractedly across the dimly lit space, the chairs near the walls seeking comfort in each other's laps. Like a dying octopus washed up on a hill of broken plates, a chandelier pointed two of its arms at the low sky. From a pile of dummy books a trail of dirty footsteps fled to the door.

Josephine's nostrils slowly widened. Bailiffs could rarely resolve cases like this to anyone's satisfaction. She would have to collect the 1,717 euros and 88 cents herself, somehow. Here and now.

When she took a step back she noticed that near her feet was another window, and that beyond it a boy in the cellar was looking dejectedly up her skirt. The blond fuzz on his chin had never been shaved, perhaps for fear it would not be replaced by a proper beard. A guitar was hanging in front of his hips. Josephine folded her arms and waited for him to look at her face. When at last he did, she pointed towards the front door.

'Are your parents home?' she asked, when the boy opened the door. Before he could answer, she slipped past him into the deserted restaurant and pattered on through what turned out to be a kitchen, a utility room and a living room, all virtually empty, steeped in dust and a sickly smell. She looked round at the boy, who had followed her.

'No,' he said. Those eyes of his. So much indignation in such a young face.

By way of a smile, Josephine briefly raised the corners of her mouth. She discovered a route back to what had been a restaurant and bent down over the pile of dummy books. Through the window she hadn't been able to see that they were damp and mildewy. She withdrew her hand and wiped it on a napkin from a supply protruding from a torn cardboard box. There was nothing to be recovered here.

Build bridges, thought Josephine, then prompt a sense of guilt; that might yet produce results.

'This can't be easy for you.'

The boy turned his eyes to the floor. 'No.'

'I noticed you play guitar?' He must have left the instrument in the cellar.

'I make hip hop,' the boy said. 'I rap, in Dutch.'

'With a guitar?' Josephine had meant to sound interested, but that wasn't how it came out. The boy flinched slightly. White stripes appeared on his reddening forehead.

'Been doing it for long?' she asked.

'No.' The white stripes slowly broadened. 'But I do plan to go on doing it for the rest of my life,' he added, with a resolve that surprised her. A dream, she thought. A child's dream.

After he'd protested rather unconvincingly against her offer to be his first audience, she followed him down the steps to the cellar, which he called his studio. There she was now, waiting on an old sofa with her legs pulled up, ready to be entertained, her empty boots side by side on the floor. It was a long time since she'd sat like that. Before starting to tune his guitar, he'd told her he was called Jake. He reminded her of someone. She couldn't think who.

Half-burned candles from the 'Nature' collection were growing out of the cellar floor. Soon she would make it clear to him that they were hers, and not yet paid for.

She didn't quite understand what she was doing in a cellar with a fourteen-year-old boy, but she couldn't imagine that Jake had any other objective in mind than to let her hear his songs. Although his attention kept wandering to her bosom, he looked away rather than back each time she caught him at it. This was a good, unhappy boy, unaware as yet of the rage couched within him.

Philip, she thought. He reminded her of Philip.

'You ought to shave,' she said, on impulse.

He pretended not to have heard and carried on tuning the same string. Josephine knew nothing about tuning guitars, but surely it wasn't supposed to take this long. Five strings to go, if he ever got the right pitch into this one.

All the same. What she was feeling wasn't exactly impatience.

'Melancholy,' said Jake.

Melancholy. Indeed. A sudden nausea came over her. When he switched the microphone on, she understood he'd merely been telling her the title. The number he'd announced began with long feedback. Once that was under control there followed a rapid, arrhythmic repetition of the same two chords.

'My rage is my world and my struggle is my way! I am a worthy worm, rejecting all constraints and wind-ups! You wanted out, I wipe you out with weirdness and revolt!'

The nasal voice assaulted her nervous system, yet she did her best not to show it. She hoped Jake would go on. The good, unhappy boy was singing about his rage after all.

'I'll wipe out anyone who wants me, 'cause what I really want is we! I'm waiting for the miracle, without weapons or protection! Wishing is my truth because the miracle awaits me!'

Why was Josephine thinking about her brother after all these years? Physically Philip didn't look at all like this humiliation-fuelled singer. It was that grim wait for a miracle, being awaited by the miracle—that must be it. Just the kind of person her brother had been.

Aside from that she hadn't understood much of the text, and she suspected Jake didn't either. The song had to do with misfortune in love, thought Josephine. The chorus consisted of the much-repeated words: 'Wretched woman! Wretched woman! Just you wait you wretched woman!'

After that Jake broke off his guitar-playing.

'That's as far as I've got,' he said.

'Ah. So it isn't finished?'

'No.'

There followed a silence in which he did his best not to ask what she thought of it and she wondered what she ought to think of it. She also thought about her brother, when he was small and she was only a little bigger, about their fanfare of spoons and lids, Philip wearing a colander for a hat, up and down the stairs, into the garden, ignoring protests, marching merrily and imperturbably, lifting their knees, awaiting the miracle.

'What did you think of it?' Jake asked after all.

'Lots of 'W's,' said Josephine.

Her answer irritated but didn't deter him.

'What did you think?'

'Good.' Why had she said that? She always steered clear of praise on principle and she hadn't even thought it was any good. Not the lyrics, anyhow, and not the way he delivered them. Although perhaps there was something in the combination of the two, something in the boy himself, the naivety and desire that were dimly visible through his anger. She was here to get her money, not to support a frustrated child.

'What exactly did you think was good about it?' he asked. His smile trembled, all his fury and protest forgotten after that minimal slap on the back from a stranger. What a lonely boy he must be; how banal of her to feel sorry for him.

'You ought to shave,' she said.

It was totally illogical and highly unprofessional of Josephine to help Jake with a parental task like his first shave. His parents had stolen from her, they owed her something. She didn't belong in their bathroom. Nevertheless she instructed Jake not to forget his throat and when he accidentally cut himself—the only razor blade they'd been able to find was quite blunt and probably meant for bikini lines— she stifled a cry of pain, an unexpected attack of empathy, a memory: Philip in the bathroom in the house where they grew up, more and more of a danger to himself. What was it that made him cut his own flesh? What was it that made him so passionately addicted?

'Haven't you got any brothers or sisters?' she asked.

'No.'

Jake tried to go on looking at himself in the bathroom mirror while splashing water on his jaws. Josephine thought she could detect a slight motor disorder.

'And your parents?'

'My mother wants to move to Luxembourg. She's there now. Looking for a house for us.'

Josephine had felt nothing but contempt for Philip's nascent self-destruction. Almost immediately she'd turned her back on him. She'd called him hopeless; others had echoed that.

With the nearest towel she wiped some foam away from below Jake's ear. She knew she would have to ask more about the mother, her role in the bankruptcy. Black money, perhaps. Luxembourg.

'You're leaving here, then?'

'Yes.' Jake said it determinedly, but also as if he regretted the move, as if it was an inescapable plan he'd assented to in another life, before he met her.

'I had a childhood dream too,' said Josephine. In the cellar she'd curled up on the sofa again. It seemed he wasn't planning to play anything else for her. He merely tickled the guitar idly around its navel as it lay on his knees. In response to her question he'd poured her a large glass of Gancia and now he was putting a bottle of beer to his lips. His smooth chin was an improvement, even though it made him look even younger. She resolutely declined the blanket he offered her and sat up straight.

She mustn't forget why she'd entered into this alliance.

It wouldn't surprise her if Mrs Cherie had kept the money

out of sight of the bailiffs by putting it into her son's bank account. Things like that did happen. The equipment he was using for his musical aspirations looked new and expensive, as did his clothes. She wanted her 1,717 euros and 88 cents. If she could get Jake to sympathize and in a flush of imagined maturity take his parents' obligations upon himself, then he could withdraw the money straight away and give it to her. She must concentrate again, this instant, leave the glass untouched.

'What do you mean, "too"?' Jake asked.

'I had a childhood dream, just like you. I wanted to be a manageress. And filthy rich.'

'Well?' he asked.

'I'm at the head of a successful company selling catering decorations. If everyone paid their bills, I'd be able to get filthy rich.' And divorced, she thought.

He didn't turn a hair, didn't even look at the half-burned candles at his feet.

'And what is my childhood dream, according to you?'

'Well … music? Isn't it?'

'No,' he said. 'That's more something from the past couple of years.'

She mustn't laugh at him.

'How old are you, actually?'

'Twenty,' he said.

She tilted her head and sent him the practised glance she'd tried out earlier on the man at the grocery shop. 'How old are you?'

Again white furrows traversed his forehead. 'Twenty,' he repeated.

It was ill luck, not bluff.

'Twenty?' she exclaimed. 'Twenty years old?' She'd made him impatient, spoilt something. She must quickly adopt the right facial expression and go on the offensive, it was her last chance. 'It's a pleasure to be dealing with an adult,' she said. 'That means I can settle this with you. Your parents owe me a sum of money. The reason I'm here …'

'How much do you need?' he interrupted her.

She could no longer fathom what was happening.

'Seventeen hundred and seventeen euros and eighty-eight cents.' She tried to sound as businesslike as possible.

'Five minutes,' he said.

He went upstairs. During his absence she must get her thoughts in order, work out whether the matter could be straightened out that easily, and if so, how. Would she wake up in a moment? Was she being lured into a trap? Might he come back with a revolver and dissolve her body in acid? She must apply logic, not think about Philip, that last summer, when she unexpectedly bumped into him beside a river in town, a handsome, sick boy of nineteen who ran towards her and held her in his arms, calling her 'sister, sister, sister' as she kept repeating that he was stoned, that he was crazy and stank, until she managed to squirm free.

'My mother left some money here for creditors.'

She looked at the tin Jake had fetched. It bore an advert for a brand of cigarette that no longer existed. He rummaged in it and counted out notes until they formed a thick pile, which Josephine awkwardly picked up.

'I don't understand,' she said, looking up at him. She seemed to annoy him. 'Why don't they pay in the normal way?'

'Is it important for you to know that?' he asked. She suddenly became aware of it: the unexpected pity that had come over her in his presence—he felt it too, for her.

'I'd like to know,' she said crossly.

'This cash is for the small bills. It's important to my mother not to feel like a monster. She wants to drag as few other small businesses as possible into her bankruptcy. Anyone who goes to a lot of trouble to recover a trivial amount of money must have a good reason, she says. It means they're desperate, so I have to pay them. There's no money for the big bills.'

Josephine needed to continue counting unperturbed, and to keep her nostrils under control. This wasn't the moment for rectifications regarding the size of her company and the existence of her desperation. As always she'd got what she came for, that was the main thing.

'You get thirty-two euros twelve back from me,' she said.

Of course the boy replied that he didn't need the change, but Josephine stood firm. She absolutely insisted on it, and when he refused to take the money she slammed it down on the coffee table, at which point all the lights went out.

It was a while before she realized there couldn't be any causal connection between what she'd done and the abrupt arrival of darkness. Only now did she notice that it was dark on the other side of the cellar window as well. Where had the day gone?

'Fuck,' said Jake. 'This is the second power cut in a week.'

He found a box of matches in one of his trouser pockets and began lighting the candles on the floor.

'I have to go,' said Josephine. She was already standing up.

'Oh,' said Jake. 'Really?'

'I came to get my money,' she said. 'What else do you want me to do here?'

There was nothing forced about her departure. There was no point continuing to sit here, staring at each other in amazement, observing how meanings leaked out of words, how emotions swapped places, how she and the boy were being blown back into their lives with the indifference of a storm.

The darkness stretched itself out over the windows, over the empty streets of the town. Josephine drove the van along them warily. This was how her brother died, driving at night. He was drunk. Traces of amphetamine were later found in his blood. Before that he'd assaulted someone. He hadn't been able to remember anything about it afterwards. The trial date had been set for a week after the crash. People said, as she did herself, that it probably wasn't an accident, that you might have seen it coming. He had it coming. Philip. Josephine had reached the slip road that led to the highway. She braked, steered onto the verge, got out and vomited. Why had she been so convinced no one could save her brother? Why hadn't she even tried?

She studied the sky fearfully. So many stars. One day one of them would incinerate the earth, she was certain of that now.

Christmas

Oh yes, the reflection in the shop window confirms it: there walks Nicolette De Puyt, seventeen and a half, sturdily built and glowing with self-reliance. She's hooked her left arm through the handle of a wicker basket, its contents covered with a red-and-white chequered tea towel that she needed to drape several times before she was satisfied with the result. As she crosses the street she can feel the wickerwork cutting into her skin through her new winter coat. It hurts a little, but the pain should make her stop to contemplate the fact that she can feel it. Gusta's left arm is paralysed. And old.

How startled she'll be, Gusta. She's not expecting Nicolette until tomorrow, on Christmas Day, still unaware that she's going to be saved from loneliness on Christmas Eve as well. Nicolette trembles slightly in the knowledge that she's about to make a difference. The happiness she'll bestow rises and radiates, baking golden-brown deep inside her. She's experienced this before, feeling turned upside down by the warmth filling her, a glow that scorches as it seeks an outlet.

Of course Gusta will behave as if she doesn't care whether anyone visits or not. She has a right to her pride. Nicolette understands. Previous visits have taught her to ignore every gruff rejection good-naturedly. Gusta's son never comes. She has little contact with the other residents of the serviced flats, mainly because she doesn't seek it. But ought this vulnerable elderly lady to be punished for her lack of social skills? Nicolette thinks not! When she first bustled determinedly into the canteen several months ago, it was Gusta who immediately caught her eye. At the end of an empty table she was rotating a chop through her mashed potato with a fork. Her limp left arm seemed stuffed with straw.

'Shall I cut up your meat?' Nicolette asked.

Gusta nodded at her with shining eyes, and after the meat had been divided into small pieces the poor woman asked her to eat it, too, since there was a nurse who would take a firm line with her if she left a whole plate of food. Nicolette first tried to convince her of the good intentions of the nurse in question and repeated several times that it was important to eat well, but when she saw that her words were making no impression on Gusta, she took one bite after another and cheerily chewed through the tough chunks of pork chop. Gusta watched, fascinated.

The start of a beautiful friendship, is how Nicolette recalls their first meeting. The hail hammers away at her cheeks for another three streets as she moves the heavy basket from one arm to the other. Then, behind a naked bush, the neon-lit canteen of the care home looms up. Between the legs of a reindeer painted with fake snow, gambolling across the big front window, she sees Gusta sitting surrounded by elderly card-players. When Nicolette taps on the windows, the others look up first, then Gusta. Nicolette points to her basket and smiles mysteriously. Inside the door her glasses fog up.

'There's your friend,' says Marcel, who is shuffling the cards. 'What's it going to be? Playing or talking?'

'If you leave us we'll be one player short. Roza's sick,' Leontine adds.

'I'm staying here,' says Gusta. 'Go ahead and deal.'

She keeps her eyes firmly on the cards in her hand, even when Nicolette puts the basket down next to the table and presses her cheek to Gusta's.

'Surprise!' she shouts in her ear.

'I thought you were coming on Christmas Day,' says Gusta. 'I'm playing cards.'

'Your turn,' says Marcel.

Gusta looks at the cards between them, then at the ones she's holding. Since she has no other usable hand, she first lays the cards face down on the table, then slides one of them out with her finger.

'Oh, but I'm coming tomorrow as well!' Nicolette enunciates. 'What a beautiful tree! Are all those presents for you?'

The old people at the surrounding tables turn their heads to look at the tree covered in blue baubles, rising out of a mountain of parcels.

'Those are empty boxes in wrapping paper,' says Gusta. 'Otherwise they'd have been stolen long ago.'

'Your turn,' says Michel.

'Wait!' says Nicolette. 'Tell me which card to play for you!'

Marcel is sweating, Gusta notices. Whenever he holds himself back he starts to sweat.

'Jack of diamonds,' she says. 'But keep your voice down, will you. I'm not deaf and I don't want to go deaf.'

'Sorry!' Nicolette shouts. After she's laid the card on the

table she walks off to look for a chair for herself. Gusta watches her go.

'So much fat on such a young girl,' she says to Marcel. 'At that age I looked rather different.'

'Isn't she a relative?' asks Leontine.

'God, no!' Gusta goes on shaking her head when Nicolette comes back to stand at the table. She hasn't found a chair.

'Your turn.' Marcel's wet forehead. His twisted mouth.

'Which do I take?' asks Nicolette, leaning down over the cards so that her young bosom rests on Gusta's neck.

Gusta continues to look at Marcel. She puts her cards down and gets up out of her chair. 'We'll go to my room,' she says gruffly.

'I've brought all kinds of things for you!' Nicolette beams, lifting her basket.

'Either we play cards or we talk, but not both together, that doesn't work!' Marcel calls after them.

Nicolette can't hide the fact that she's excited about being invited into Gusta's serviced flat for the first time. All things considered, it hasn't taken her long to gain the woman's trust. The broad smile with which she steps out of the lift wavers as she takes in the room. It's neat but small and austere, far too austere. Not a single photo has been stuck up on the low walls. That damn loneliness, thinks Nicolette.

'I've brought all sorts of things for you,' she repeats.

Gusta sinks into an adjustable chair and watches dejectedly as Nicolette puts four Tupperware boxes, a bottle of Worldshake, a candelabra and coloured candles on the small table.

'No wine?' she asks.

'You know very well it's not allowed,' Nicolette replies. That finger.

She still hasn't quite emptied the basket. Gusta wants to scream when she sees the plastic Christmas tree. All she can manage is, 'Oh dear.'

'Christmas!' Nicolette blares over her. As she spreads the branches of wire and green shreds she peers purposefully around the room. She opts for the top of the television. Then she winds a far-too-long string of fairy lights around the tree, the plug of which has to go into the socket for the TV.

'There's a programme I want to watch,' Gusta grumbles.

'What time?'

'Around eight.'

Gusta's watch broke last week. She ought to have got it repaired straight away. Outside it's dark, but according to Nicolette it's only half past five and they have plenty of time to talk and eat.

'It's lucky you have a microwave!' she says. In the kitchenette she discovers plates in a cupboard. 'I've brought a cold starter, but we do need to heat up the main course.'

'I'm not all that hungry,' says Gusta.

'Wait till you see it! Do you have a tablecloth?'

'No,' Gusta lies.

She has to admit that she likes the starter. Something with salmon mousse and mashed sprouts.

'Is that what you ate at home too?' she asks.

'No, I bought it in the supermarket.' Nicolette seems to regard this as a shortcoming on her part and quickly adds: 'I made the salad myself.'

Gusta peers at her between two burning candles.

'Your parents must be sorry you're not home on Christmas Eve.'

'Oh, but my mother and her boyfriend aren't there themselves,' Nicolette laughs. 'They were definitely ready for a holiday. Insane how hard they work. I hope they're enjoying themselves in Rome. A chance to completely de-stress.'

Gusta senses she shouldn't ask about the father, but once the Worldshake has neutralized the taste of salmon in her mouth she asks nonetheless.

'I haven't seen him for a long time,' Nicolette answers. Then she abruptly claps her hands and announces with lorry-loads of good cheer that they must turn off the chandelier. Only the Christmas lights can stay on. She acts on that proclamation straight away and concludes it was a good step: combined with the candles, the fairy lights make a huge contribution to the atmosphere.

Oh no, thinks Gusta. Not now. A slightly clumsy move and she's down on the floor between toilet and washbasin. This has never happened before. The soft bathroom mat has broken her fall, nothing seems to hurt, it's just that somehow she can't get up. Although she has often said you can adjust to anything, she curses her paralysed arm now, and the stroke that left her with it. She'd still be living in her own home otherwise. Feeding her rabbits. There'd be no seventeen-year-old busybody standing at the bathroom door.

'Gusta, what was that noise?'

'It's nothing.'

'Did you have a fall?'

'I'm on the toilet! Stay there!'

'I think you've had a fall! I'll have to come in, Gusta! If you're not out in one minute I'm coming in!'

Gusta tries to curl her spine and rock herself upwards. She pushes with her good arm, but it refuses to take her weight. She doesn't dare let go of the floor to try for a handhold higher up. This body is hers. It smarts at her exertions. It relies on her for help.

'I'm here!' shouts Nicolette. This is doubtless a red-letter day for her. Sixty-eight kilos of defenceless old lady on the floor. Gusta can't understand how she could have forgotten to lock the door.

'First we need to check that no vital functions are affected,' says Nicolette as she kneels down beside Gusta.

'I don't care how many first aid courses you've done! If you're so determined to help me, let me lean on you so I can stand up!'

When Nicolette, slightly thrown now for the first time, does as she's asked, Gusta shouts: 'My other arm!'

By bumping against Gusta's shoulder, or because of the way she bends forward, Nicolette loses her glasses. They slide off her nose and land next to the bathroom mat.

'I'm up now,' Gusta says. While Nicolette retrieves her glasses, she walks out of the bathroom. She doesn't need glasses herself.

She yanks the fairy-light plug out of the socket and re-places it with the one for the TV. She can zap around until the child leaves. Hoping embarrassment might speed her departure, she lingers at a sex scene. A beautiful naked man and a beautiful naked woman roll intertwined from the bed onto the carpet. Then they descend the stairs panting and slurping.

'I do understand,' says Nicolette.

When Gusta looks round despite herself, one seventeen-year-old eye is gazing patiently at her. The other is hidden behind multiple cracks.

'I understand,' Nicolette says again. 'Your pride has taken a knock, even though there's no need for that at all. It's only me. And you're up again now. It's just one of those things. You simply have to accept it. It's perfectly normal to have a fall at your age.'

She goes on to add this and that, about how Gusta might fall again, about being prepared and always carrying a mobile phone that has her number in it. But Gusta has stopped listening. She opens a window and throws the fairy-light-wrapped tree through it. The empty plates—the main course wasn't bad, partridge—soon follow.

'You're old, do you realize that?!' Gusta shouts. 'Why else are you here? With your finger food and your bosoms, your way of moving and your voice. You're old!' She enjoys tossing the objects into the air with her good hand for a moment, then lifting them above her head and flinging them with all her strength down through the window. With her good eyes she can see shards bouncing up off the pavement.

When she finally turns to look, Nicolette's chair is empty. She won't be back, thinks Gusta. She shuts the window and waits for a sense of relief.

At home Nicolette feeds the cats. Her mother has taken in seven. She knows her daughter will care for them conscientiously, you can rely on her for that.

The optical effect of the broken lens multiplies the number of cats. There are too many of them, thinks Nicolette.

She picks up the phone and keys in a Rome hotel phone number that she wrote on a Post-it a week ago.

'I will check their room, Madam,' a receptionist says with an Italian accent.

During the cheery 'Funiculi Funicula' of the on-hold music, it occurs to Nicolette that he didn't call her 'Miss'.

'They are out, Madam,' says the receptionist, and, as if deliberately trying to dramatize his message, he adds: 'There is nobody.'

No doubt there's a good reason why her mother hasn't rung, a reason that for the duration of one bright flash Nicolette couldn't care less about, couldn't feel less comforted by; she feels a fury rising that's new to her. Her mind casts about in a wide open space. She feels totally paralysed. The house is dirty and empty. Perhaps she ought to have bought a Christmas tree for herself. No, Nicolette quickly thinks, she'll forgive everyone, it's the lens.

With the back of a steak knife she carefully digs out the fragments of broken glass. When she holds the glasses close to her face she notices that the frames are damaged too. It's only a pair of spectacles. It's only a feeling, only a young life, only a Nicolette. She's still some way short of becoming an adult. A lot may change yet, or simply happen.

As she cleans the house she keeps bumping into things. She has no proper sense of depth. She shuts one eye, then the other, but it doesn't help.

She carries on wiping and scrubbing until midnight, finding a box of Christmas decorations in the process and adorning the bookcase with them. When she looks at the results from various angles, something about the picture changes again. It blurs and seems to bulge a little. Nicolette realizes that this time it's because of her tears.

At five in the morning Gusta is woken by a call from her son, who wishes her a happy Christmas and asks whether all's well with her.

'Extremely well,' says Gusta.

'Were you still asleep? What time is it there?'

'Eight o'clock. I've been up for a while already. How are you doing?'

'Fine.'

After that they both cast around for a subject. Gusta remembers a chequered winter coat. He was about five when he wore it, his mittens on a cord through the sleeves. His red nose. A flake of snow that settled on his eyelashes. The way he ate waffles, folded double. She can't make out the child in the voice in her ear, but its loss silences her.

'You sure everything's all right?'

'Oh yes.'

'And your health?'

'Well, this arm you know.'

'Be glad your leg's working again. You were lucky.'

'Yes.'

Perhaps he senses that she's controlling herself, that she doesn't like to ask, because he says: 'I really wanted to come and visit but I just couldn't. It's so busy here.'

'In the summer then, probably?'

'I'll see what I can do. Are you going to have a nice lunch with the others?'

'Yes, there's some kind of party this afternoon.'

'Have fun there then.'

'Thanks. What are you going to do?'

'Someone's coming to cook for me at home.'

'Oh.'

'No, not what you think. Just a friend who's good with food. Company.'

'Yes.'

'I'm expecting her at any moment so I'd better hang up. Have fun there, Mum.'

'Bye, Tony. Call soon.'

'Will do.'

'Kisses.'

Gusta takes a shower right away. She won't be able to get back to sleep, the day will just have to last longer. She puts on something festive because yesterday's clothes remind her of the fall, the throwing. The silk shirt was never meant for Marcel, not the slightest bit. He's got something going with Leontine; she isn't blind.

The Tupperware boxes are still in the kitchen. She makes the pedal bin open its mouth but then she washes them after all and stores them away in the furthest corner she can find in the small cupboard. Just company, Tony said.

She tries to read. When she hears that the day has begun for the other residents too, she takes the lift down and bumps into Marcel's family. He's issuing instructions in an authoritarian tone. His son nods at Gusta and she nods back. His daughter is walking arm in arm with Leontine—she's allowed to go with them; she belongs with them now.

In the afternoon there's a party for those left behind. The tombola presents Gusta with a breadboard. She declines dessert and is the first to leave.

In her room she opens the window. The Christmas tree and crockery shards have been cleared away. The Tupperware boxes are standing ready. She has no way to reach her, that stupid, stupid, adorable girl.

The day after Christmas, Nicolette finds an optician's that's open. She produces her glasses and gives the strength of the lens.

'The frame is a bit damaged too,' says the man.

'That doesn't matter,' says Nicolette.

'Haven't you ever considered contact lenses?' he asks.

'I want the same glasses,' says Nicolette tersely. She's thought about this. Her mind is made up.

Pioneer

'It's not because we can't see it that it's not there.'

Professor Ignaz Semmelweis ran his eyes along the row of faces at the long table: doctors' faces, most of them pale, outdoors framed by high hats and fur collars, indoors by white fabrics that were often spattered. Unbelieving faces, tired and grave, malevolent and immaculate, infuriatingly shortsighted, above all the latter. Positivists. There were some who supported him, inwardly, Ignaz knew that. He had spoken with restraint. He must keep that up. Begin at the beginning. Convince them. No one said anything.

'As a young man I initially studied law,' he began, already feeling rather moved by his own words because he knew what was to follow. 'After a year I switched to medicine, because I wanted to help people more directly. I wanted to help them with the most important thing of all: staying alive.'

'Professor Semmelweis.'

Doctor Braun looked as stern as he could while suppressing a yawn. His persecutor, his demon. Ignaz decided against the dramatic pauses he'd been intending to let fall. He quickly continued. 'When I started working at the First Obstetric Clinic of the General Hospital in Vienna, deaths following childbirth were at their peak, in contrast to the Second Obstetric Clinic at the same hospital. Women who were having contractions fell at my feet, begging me …'

'Professor Semmelweis.'

'Begging me to have them taken to the Second Clinic, the one with the midwives. Some even chose to give birth out on the street. More than once, when I was on duty a few days later I would watch the life drain out of one of those women, leaving behind the life she had bestowed on the world, motherless.'

'Professor …'

There was a sound of muttering and fidgeting. Ignaz Semmelweis talked over it.

'No! I promised myself and those pitiful souls that I wouldn't let these atrocious cases of childbed fever make life seem worthless any longer, I wouldn't allow it! What was the secret of the Second Clinic? Why was the death rate there so much lower? I investigated everything. Was it the way clothes were ironed? Was it the diet? What were the students at the First Clinic doing differently from the midwives of the Second?'

'Ignaz.'

'But then: ah! A sacrifice. It was the death of my closest friend, that good man Jakob Kolletschka. A sacrifice. Jakob died a few days after a student accidentally poked him with a scalpel during an autopsy. When I studied the cadaver, Jakob's body, I recognized the pathology immediately. It was a revelation. This was what childbed fever looked like! And I understood: the infections did not originate in the body, nor did they float down onto it out of the sky, they came …'

'Ignaz!'

Ignaz Semmelweis woke from the trance he always fell

into while reliving the discovery. Most of the faces around the table looked morose, two of them potentially compassionate.

'We know all this already, Ignaz.'

Of course they knew it all already, here and in Vienna. And they also knew he was right. It had been proven in practice.

Doctor Braun held out his hands. There was nothing special about them. Ignaz Semmelweis looked right into the eyes of the man who had twice taken his place.

'Itch,' was all Doctor Braun said.

His assistant nodded angrily and started scratching the palms of his own hands.

Not again, thought Ignaz. In Vienna it was Doctor Klein who had thwarted him, and eventually got him replaced by Doctor Braun. Klein had meanwhile dispensed with handwashing. The young women in his department were dying like flies.

Sometimes Ignaz wondered whether the evidence for his assertion might be accepted if it was substantiated by a different man, someone they liked. They were willing to deploy tens of thousands of dead to obstruct him. How many lives could he have saved if he hadn't been Ignaz Semmelweis? How many hours of sleep had that agonizing thought cost him?

He must keep on trying. He had to call himself a professor but he was still a doctor; he'd made life a solemn promise and to keep it he must learn to converse calmly, in a businesslike manner, to the point of subservience if necessary.

'Chlorine can cause slight irritation, but that's as nothing compared to the huge reduction in mortality that's been recorded here in Pest just as it was in Vienna. During the first few years that I worked as a doctor at St Rochus, hand-washing practically eliminated deaths following childbirth.'

'And afterwards they went up again. There is no evidence, Professor Semmelweis.'

Gradually more women had started dying again. He suspected his colleagues of having deliberately spread the infection, to prove him wrong. There was no evidence for that, either.

'When I first walked in here, Doctor Braun, I found four seriously ill women, one dying and one a corpse! That's as many cases of childbed fever as in all the subsequent five years put together. What do you mean, no evidence? You can't go on saying that!'

They could. The look on Braun's face told him he hadn't the slightest doubt that they could.

'Cadaverous particles, Ignaz?'

As Braun said it, Ignaz became aware that he'd picked the wrong term. Cadaverous particles. It sounded almost magical, something from a gothic novel. He'd always struggled with words, especially German words. That was why it had taken him so long to publish anything. He also had a tendency to repeat himself, and in his second book especially it had been a great effort to sustain a scientific tone. Too many exclamation marks. Too many personal attacks. As if he'd wanted to convince his enemies he was unstable. It had aroused too much indignation. He couldn't turn back the clock.

The fact that Doctor Braun didn't speak a word of Hungarian had been greeted with protest initially. Since then, everyone had adjusted to him.

'Please, don't become fixated upon that term. It's not about what we choose to call them. What matters is that we know they're there, we can smell them, and we carry them on our hands and instruments from the cadavers to the women.'

'Don't worry, Professor Semmelweis, we are well aware of the theory you're putting into the heads of your students. You've managed to extract compliance from this department and for several years now we've been wasting a great deal of our time washing away some sort of invisible but highly dangerous substance.'

Doctor Braun's assistant broke into a nervous laugh.

'You surely aren't considering giving up the habit?'

'What we are obliged to do, Professor Semmelweis, what should or should not be part of our daily practice is—however improbable this may seem to you—not your decision. Have you ever considered the fact that several of the doctors in this department regard it as an insult to be compelled to wash their hands?'

Ignaz had considered that fact. When implementing the hygiene measures several had grunted that they felt themselves treated like children. They too were sitting at this table.

'No social class is impervious to cadaverous particles!'

He expected this exclamation to lead to fierce protest, imagined that the most ardent of his listeners might throw a chair. A man who had once been dismissed under political pretexts was supposed to stay well away from issues of class. A grocer's son would do well to keep silent about them in any case.

The commotion was not forthcoming. Instead the faces

folded themselves into caricatures of fatherly concern, expressing every conceivable combination of resentment towards and empathy for their degenerate son.

Doctor Braun still seemed to be the only one with a voice.

'Professor Semmelweis … Ignaz, tomorrow a busy working day, with great responsibilities, awaits us all.'

Ignaz managed to limit his reaction on hearing the word 'responsibilities' to the sucking-in of his lips.

'May we sum up this meeting, in conclusion, by stating that you continue to encourage the washing of hands with chlorine but thus far have not managed to commit to paper any new evidence for the existence of "cadaverous particles"?'

Ignaz Semmelweis bowed his head. Around him oak chairs were pushed away from the table. The doctors would now comb their moustaches before being driven through the evening streets of Pest, to their families.

Ignaz ought to go home too, if only to put his wife's mind at rest, but he walked in the other direction, away from the gloom that awaited him there. He had not brought Maria any happiness, instead he'd transformed her in no time at all from a coquettish twenty-year-old into a mourning pietà. Their first child had died almost immediately, the second clung to life for four months. Horror-struck, Maria had exhorted him to do something, to turn their fate around; he was a doctor, wasn't he? The fact that, after those little coffins, he'd given her another two daughters and a son, three sickly children who were easily bored, had done nothing to stave off her rejection of him.

He couldn't face her straight after the renewed derision at St Rochus. What had he been expecting? How could he have had the nerve to try again? His Open Letters had been the final straw, desperate, abusive diatribes aimed at the doctors who had rebuked him all over Europe. On page after page he'd called them murderers. He'd written that they were epidemics themselves. After that no one had tried very hard to make sense of his theories, which he hadn't managed to clarify anyway. He'd botched all his chances. It was over.

Ignaz stopped walking and watched the Danube at his feet, which he'd been following, for how long?—lost in thought. It was as if he and the current had been keeping pace with each other, as if the river had silently stayed at his side. Now he allowed it to continue on its course from the Black Forest to the Black Sea, past his black heart.

On the far side of the water St Matthias Church adorned the skyline of Buda. When the Turks destroyed one of the church walls in the late seventeenth century, a statue of the Virgin Mary was revealed: Muslims on their knees; city saved; endless mass devotion for a bricked-up doll. But you make a discovery that saves hundreds of people right there and then, with the potential to spare millions of future lives a horrible end, and they don't believe you.

Little of substance had changed since the seventeenth century, Ignaz decided. He couldn't muster it any more, philanthropy. He'd once believed in humanity, progress, independence for the Hungarians. But there was no such thing as revolution, a liberated people or general betterment; there was only a stupid, shrieking beast that distributed itself equitably among all human beings and lashed out wildly time and again.

It was lodged within Ignaz too, that beast, he knew it was, and when it manifested itself he no longer tried to resist. Often it emerged, as now, in the form of a wistful contemplation, combined with a deep emotional response to the truth he'd discovered. That was followed by a barrage of humiliating memories, to which he could add this afternoon. The issue of his own responsibility, the realization that a different, more likeable man would have been capable of persuasion and therefore of saving others, arose again too. But there was something worse than any of that. What made the beast really ferocious was the possibility that he might be mistaken.

The beast usually led Ignaz down a trail of bars and brothels. In the bars he drank too much and spoke drunkenly to young couples in love. He told them how they could avoid having children, spared them none of the disgusting details in his description of childbed fever, and made them solemnly promise to instruct the doctors to wash their hands. He bought the couples drinks, so they listened at first. After the listening came the threats, and after the threats came Ignaz' departure. Sometimes they shouted after him that they weren't the ones who needed to watch out, he was. Even in those places, pity usually prevented a punch-up.

The streets between the bars of his native city became increasingly long and unfamiliar. Sometimes they turned out to be dead ends. Sometimes he imagined himself followed by gangs of toughs led by Doctor Braun and Doctor Klein.

The girl he visited most often called him doctor. She hid his hat as soon as he came in and stroked his bald head. After he'd given his distress free rein on top of her and sobbed for a while afterwards in her arms, she caressed him again. Perhaps she didn't realize he was weeping out of fear; one day she would bear an unwanted child in St Rochus, where they'd all stopped washing their hands. A number of times he'd been so drunk he couldn't remember afterwards whether he'd taken his precautions. The child that caused her death might be his.

To allay that fear, Ignaz usually drank even more, which drove him onwards again, made him return to his starting point, his discovery, made him decide he must not give up the fight. He was right. They'd eventually see that, because he was.

'Listen carefully, my turtle doves.'

They were the same age as Maria when she became his wife, less than seven years ago, even though she looked a good twenty years older now.

'Listen carefully to Doctor Semmelweis! Doctor Semmelweis says you must be extremely cautious about having children and he'll explain to you why that is! It's the doctors, youngsters—they carry death on their hands! Cadaverous particles, children, remember that term: cadaverous particles!'

He hissed the 'S' at the end for a long time and wiggled his fingertips close to their faces. As he did so he was forced to perform a series of tight little dance steps to keep his balance. When he grabbed hold of them, they called the police.

It wasn't the first time these two policemen had bundled him into a carriage. Even the horses seemed to recognize him, stamping impatiently until the door was locked. Their canter sounded as if they wanted to be rid of him as quickly as possible.

'My dear Professor Semmelweis. Respect for your honourable profession is great but not inexhaustible. You must take care.'

In the darkness he was unable to make out the officer who had said it. He imagined the dirt under the man's nails. He turned away from the voice, opened his sore eyes wide, facing the place where the windows must be and beyond them the unrecognizable city hurtling past. There had been several years, shortly after his return to Pest, in which he'd turned his back on science, delightful years when he sang and danced. He could hear leaves scraping the roof of the carriage, cracking twigs, the beast running off into the wilderness. Then nothing but the sound of the river. Happiness cut right through him. The Danube would never come to a standstill.

Fever, thought Ignaz, this too is fever.

'There he is, the saviour of mothers!'

Although he couldn't see Maria, Ignaz knew she was standing at the top of the stairs, looking down at him with loathing. It was a long time since the supporters of handwashing, several of his students and former teachers, had called him that: the saviour of mothers.

'Just go to sleep, Maria.'

He heard her storm down the stairs as he walked towards the salon. He'd been planning to feel his way to a jug of water before going to bed, but Maria lit an oil lamp. It seemed she wanted to be able to see him when starting an argument.

She was wearing a crumpled nightgown and had not taken the trouble to put her hair up. The beast seemed to be lodged in her as well tonight. It was looking out of her eyes, untameable. Then it came to stand close and started snuffling him thoroughly.

'Little children!' she called out. 'Father is stewed again and he smells of whore!'

'Shut your mouth!'

Upstairs the baby began to cry. The older children must be awake now too.

She was about to shout something else. Ignaz put one hand over her mouth and used the other to squeeze her throat shut. Over the past few years there had been several scenes like this, contorted fights in which she hit him in the chest with hard little fists or sank her claws into his cheeks and he pulled her hair until she fell silent. It was the things she said, the strange conclusions that slipped out of her after she'd been forced to observe him for too long. Like tonight, when she shouted that he had more and more of a stoop. It was true. It must be the weight of the world.

Then, after a fight, or even as a transition between two tussles: an embrace. Usually he clutched her; tonight it was the other way around.

'Forgive me, Ignaz.'

'You haven't done anything wrong.'

Ignaz Semmelweis lay on the rug between the sofa and the coffee table, his thin wife in his arms. Before she stopped crying, he fell asleep.

He'd never before had the experience of waking up in a moving carriage with no memory of a departure. For the first few seconds he assumed he was still dreaming. His wife, whom he noticed sitting next to him, reinforced that assumption. She looked beautiful, dressed in a fashionable frock that he'd never seen before. Her made-up face regarded him serenely and she stroked his bald head the way he was used to with his girl.

'We're on a trip,' she said. 'To Vienna.'

He felt the wind blowing on his neck through the gaps around the door. Awake. Maria became conscious that he was trying to sit up straight to ask questions and she put her finger to his lips.

'Yesterday a letter arrived for you, Ignaz. I opened it because it looked important. It's from Ferdinand Ritter von Hebra, the famous dermatologist! He writes that he admires you and wants your help in one of his new institutes. That's where we're going. On holiday. So that you can meet him and we can prepare for the move.'

She spoke merrily, girlishly cheerful to the point of insanity.

'Please, Ignaz. No questions.'

Hadn't she fallen asleep crying in his arms last night, on the rug? Who was looking after the children?'

She gave him the letter, which he cursorily read. Hebra. Ignaz had met him when he was working in Vienna, but he couldn't remember anything more than a superficial conversation. Could Hebra have been on his side all this time and taken up his cause without his knowledge? Had the time of the helpers arrived? How did he come to be in this luxurious carriage? Was it memory loss?

Maria kept ignoring his questions, saying he must let things take their course, that he must learn to enjoy himself again. Her voice sounded different. Her mouth was strangely wide when she laughed. Along the way they ate in restaurants that in the past she would have found too expensive, and the same went for the hotel where they spent the night. She had a tailor make a suit for him, kept repeating that he must straighten his back, must look good, for her, for Hebra. Was she trying to save their marriage? Had their marriage been saved?

During the final few kilometres he no longer thought in questions but simply listened to the clatter of hoofs and to his wife's new laugh.

A pale, unpleasant light shone on Vienna. However much Maria tried to distract him, Ignaz kept looking out through the window to see where they were going. With rising horror he realized he could predict every bend, every turn. When they drove into the Lazarettgasse, he threw himself at the door, which was bolted on the outside.

'It's for your own good. I did it for you,' Maria squeaked.

It took the nurses quite some time to prise his fingers from her throat.

In the last twenty days of his life he was severely beaten each time he tried to escape. Despite the straitjacket, he contracted an infection that caused symptoms resembling those of childbed fever. Perhaps he'd managed to bite a dead patient, and then himself.

Much remained for ever hidden from Ignaz Semmelweis: Louis Pasteur, his son's suicide and two world wars. He would never hear the news that a museum was to be named after him, or that his likeness was to feature on a postage stamp, and on a commemorative coin.

Potpourri

The first time Wolf went to visit Roman and Andreas—they were celebrating their fifth birthday—his mother said, 'Good afternoon' to the twins' mother in a tone of voice that indicated Wolf should say the same. Before he could open his mouth, Roman and Andreas' mother answered: 'Hello, Wolf. Just call me Tatiana.' For a moment Wolf's mother said nothing and he thought that she, like him, was captivated by the woman's voice.

Their house smelled good. It struck him even before he saw some of the children from his class sitting round the table.

'You can't give them your present yet,' said one. 'We're first.'

'Hi Wolf,' said Roman. With a wild tug he ripped the paper from a large parcel. This upset his brother, who would have preferred to ease off the tape so that the paper stayed nice and could be kept.

'Wolf, would you like a Coke?' asked Tatiana. He looked up at her. She seemed to mean it. Mum said you had to be crazy to drink something that could be used to clean rusty nails.

'Or would you prefer chocolate milk?'

He nodded.

'Hot?'

He nodded again. Her eyes were light green, her eyelids light blue.

'You've got a big television!' said Smilla, one of the children at the table. 'But my uncle's is even bigger!'

Wolf didn't believe Smilla. This must surely be the biggest television you could possibly get. Mum said only stupid people had huge televisions. Perhaps that didn't apply to twins. Or to people with light-green eyes.

On top of the dresser over by the wall was a small wooden box. Wolf recognized a stronger version of the smell that had attracted him just now. He carefully lifted the lid, which had holes in it. Down inside lay dried yellow flowers, nuts and pips. Bits of banana, too, like the ones in his father's muesli.

'Wolf's touching everything!' Smilla shouted.

Even Roman and Andreas looked up from the Lego fishing boat they'd just freed from its paper with great difficulty and much squabbling.

Wolf felt his body swelling with tears. If he wasn't to wet his pants, they would have to come out through his eyes.

'That's potpourri.' He had no idea what Tatiana meant, but she looked friendly as she said it and she came over to stand between him and the children. 'Smells good, doesn't it Wolf?'

Nodding, he put the lid back in place.

'Here you go,' said Tatiana.

He took the cup from her. She briefly smoothed his hair.

Several other children hopped off their chairs and ran over to investigate the little box. Tatiana held it under each nose for precisely the same length of time.

'Oh, I've known all about that for ages,' said Smilla. 'We've got lots of those boxes at home. I've known about it for a hundred years.'

Wolf put the cup to his lips. As the sweetest chocolate milk he'd ever tasted warmed his mouth, throat and stomach, a new, supple sensation climbed up his ribs.

During the drive home, his mother said Tatiana had an accent.

'Has she lost her toes?' asked Wolf. An accent had to be a hidden defect. Tatiana still had her legs and arms. Her fingers too. Tiny stars were painted on her long, pink-lacquered nails, shiny, beautiful. He hadn't seen her feet; they were in high purple boots. Maybe she'd lost her toes in an accident with an electric saw. He suddenly felt truly sorry for her.

'What did you say? Lost her toes?'

Wolf pointed at the road in front of them. Mum mustn't look at him like that while she was driving.

'Do you know what that is? An accent?'

He shook his head, hoping she wouldn't ask any more about Tatiana's toes and pointed at the road again, with emphasis.

'That mammee of Rrroman and Andrrreas comes from White Rrroossiah, that's why she talks like that.'

'Not true!' He gave his mother a fierce look.

'She does. She's from White Russia. That's next to ordinary Russia.'

'She doesn't talk like that!'

'It was a joke, Wolf!' Mum was now concentrating firmly on the road. 'Don't be so serious always.'

Wolf knew this kind of silence. For a long time he looked

at the small bushes at the roadside, which were relentlessly attacked by the wind and bravely fought back. Above them the white clouds were transformed into Tatiana's snow-covered country.

On schooldays Mum was off to work by the time Wolf woke up. As on every other morning, he heard his father creep into the room, climb onto a chair and throw himself into a cry of 'Cock-a-doodle-do!'

Wolf usually woke before the morning ritual but, however painfully badly he needed to go to the toilet, he always pretended he was still asleep.

'Oh, Daddy!' he said, giggly and startled, after every cock-a-doodle-do. As he said it he laid his hand on his chest and rolled his eyes. His father deserved that much. He had fourteen allergies and often worked until after midnight.

'Does my hair stink, Wolf?' Dad asked at breakfast with his mouth full of muesli. 'I have the impression my hair stinks.' He held his ponytail under his nose and sniffed. Wolf's mother didn't like long hair. If it started to stink, she'd definitely want to take the scissors to it against his will. She'd already threatened to.

Wolf sprang up from his chair and walked to the other side of the table. His father leaned over and he sniffed at the hair with great concentration. He didn't actually know what hair was supposed to smell like, so he said it did stink a bit, which was true, in the way that most things stink a bit.

'I'd better just give it a wash.'

'Yes.' Wolf was thinking about something. 'Do you know what smells good?'

'Fabric softener?' his father guessed.

'Potpourri.'

'That too, yes.'

Dad was someone you could talk to.

Roman and Andreas called out to him as he walked into the playground. Wolf couldn't recall them ever having done that before. Perhaps it had to do with the board game he'd given them for their birthday, although yesterday afternoon they'd found it too difficult and hadn't played to the end.

The twins actually ran towards him. They were wearing identical chequered shirts.

'Mum says you can come and play with us any time,' said Andreas. Roman looked at him impassively.

Tatiana had said he could come back. Any time.

'Okay,' said Wolf. 'I can come this evening. I can stay the night.'

The twins took stock of each other briefly and Andreas said they'd ask.

Wolf's day was full of sunlight and victories. Through the window next to the red table set aside for drawing he watched black birds dancing high in the air in a circle. He set them down on paper as accurately as he could.

At first the teacher encouraged him to use other colours too, but when he showed her what he was looking at and re-assured her that the background would of course be as blue as the sky, she called his drawing 'so original'.

After he'd been the only one to remember all the words of a song they'd been taught the day before and the last one left at the end of musical chairs, the school day was finally over.

His mother arrived before Tatiana. Impatient and pleased in equal measure, she listened to what the teacher had to say about her son. She no doubt found it less irritating than she claimed when Wolf pulled her along with him after he spotted the twins and their mother outside.

'I can sleep at Roman and Andreas' house tonight. Tatiana said I could,' Wolf informed his mother as they ran.

'No, not tonight,' said his mother. She nodded, smiling, to Tatiana.

'Another time,' said Tatiana, before his face could crumple. 'Roman and Andreas would like that, I'm sure.'

The twins stood watching as if they'd no idea what all this was about. Wolf felt an urge to throw himself to the ground. He'd done it before, making himself into a lead cannonball that his mother then had to struggle to move. But now Tatiana was around.

'I've got something for you,' she said. The thing she pulled out of the pocket of her leather jacket looked like a pillow for a Barbie. The scent wafted up at him as he took it in both hands.

'Potpourri,' Tatiana explained. 'He likes it.'

'Oh, really?' His mother smiled a little to make her reaction sound less defensive.

He walked all the way to the car backwards, so that he could wave as long as possible.

His mother didn't like potpourri. She thought it was something for old ladies in small, dark houses, a type of kitsch she was keen to avoid. She also had something against the word, because it sounded chic but meant stew and was used for any old hodgepodge. When Wolf spread the dried flowers and seeds out over the table, she spoke in a high-pitched voice about microbes and dye. She insisted the new smell filling the room was more like toilet duck than flowers.

'You've made clear what you think,' his father said, unusually vehement. She leaned back on the frame of the door to Wolf's bedroom and looked at her husband and son, who were lying side by side in Wolf's high bed, reading a story and taking turns to sniff deeply at the handkerchief full of potpourri. From time to time her quick thumb typed long text messages on the buttons of her phone. They didn't ask to whom.

At the end of the next school day he was again unable to go with the twins. They were picked up by their father.

'What an ugly man,' said his mother.

Wolf had to agree. The man had a small, bald head with so many furrows it looked shrunken. His eyes were in proportion, but the nose, mouth, ears and throat seemed to belong to a larger face. Wolf felt afraid of him instantly and wanted that man to stay right away from Tatiana.

'They're divorced,' he said.

'Yes,' Mum said. 'Makes sense.'

Motionless, they watched Roman and Andreas' father push them rather roughly in the direction of a polished car. He twisted his shapeless body to one side as he walked.

'A Jaguar,' said his mother. She meant the car.

When they stopped at the same traffic lights as the Jaguar, Roman and Andreas puffed out their cheeks against the window. Their father nodded politely to Wolf's mother.

'Bye-bye ugly rich man,' she said without altering her smile. 'Well spotted, Tatiana.' She refused to explain what she meant by that, even when Wolf asked her for the third time.

At dinner that evening she couldn't stop explaining. To his father, though.

'Of course you can hardly blame her. Who knows, I might well let myself get impregnated by the ugliest millionaire in the Western world if I didn't have enough to eat and had been abused by half my family, or God knows what she's been through. Still. No. I couldn't do it. To think that a man like that marries without realizing it isn't going to last. Incredible, isn't it? How can you get that rich if you're so gullible? You should just see how she lives, what she wears.'

'Maybe he was the one who left her,' said Dad. 'Men with a lot of power get fed up with things more quickly, even of the most beautiful women.'

'How do you know that?' his mother asked. When his father didn't answer she added: 'She's not all that beautiful anyhow.'

'Yes she is!' Wolf exclaimed.

His parents turned to look at him. Wolf closed his eyes, covered his nostrils with the potpourri-stuffed handkerchief, sniffed and sniffed and pretended not to hear his mother attributing addictive properties to the dried flowers and speculating aloud about all the damage it could do.

He had to wait until the Wednesday afternoon of the following week before he was allowed to go and visit the twins.

'He's not to have any lactose at all,' his mother said to Tatiana at the front door. 'He's inherited his father's allergies. I've brought some chocolate soya milk for him. After the birthday party he had diarrhoea all week.'

'That's not true!' Wolf tugged himself free.

Tatiana laid her hand on his hair. 'Just go on inside,' she said. 'The boys are waiting for you.'

Roman and Andreas had a racing track that three remote-controlled cars could drive on at the same time. Because they seemed mainly interested in ramming each other's cars, Wolf won most of the races. After that they played the same game on their computer.

The warm playroom made Wolf feel sleepy. He lay for a while on a huge cushion with his legs and arms stretched out as the twins carried on playing.

'Is it all right if I go downstairs for a bit?' he asked eventually.

Andreas nodded and shrugged, then turned back to the game and repeated his brother's name several times in a plaintive voice, with mounting incomprehension.

Tatiana was working in the garden. He could see her through the big glass doors next to the sofas. She was wearing green gloves and rubber boots. There were smears of dirt on her bare arms. She'd bunched her hair up under a cap. Cautiously he opened the door.

'Hello,' he said.

'Hi Wolf,' said Tatiana. 'Don't you feel like playing any more?'

She pushed her index finger into the soil until Wolf could no longer see it.

'I'm planting beans. Runner beans.'

'What's that plastic bag for?'

'I wind it around a stick and then push it into the ground. Like this.'

Wolf watched Tatiana planting seeds around the stick and burying the edges of the bag in the soil.

'A tent.' He went and knelt down next to her and did as she was doing.

'Thank you, Wolf! Roman and Andreas would never do that.'

'My mother doesn't do it either,' he said. 'We don't have a garden.'

'But you've got green fingers,' she said. 'Like me.' She laughed when he fleetingly glanced at his hands and went on: 'We like grubbing about in the soil.' She pulled off her gloves, made claws and attacked the ground.

Wolf buried his own hands until they were completely invisible. Under the soil their twenty fingers were the legs of a squirming animal no one could catch. When the animal grew calmer, he touched one of Tatiana's nails. He stroked the stars drawn on it and then the whole finger. She laughed nervously for a moment. Then her hand became a spider that crawled up out of the brown earth. Wolf jerked back and she showed him her soil-smeared fingers, right up close to his face, so he could be certain there wasn't really a spider.

'Did Roman and Andreas' dad go away?' he asked.

She turned her green eyes to him calmly. 'We don't live together any longer,' she said. 'You know that, don't you?'

'But did *he* go?'

'You don't need to concern yourself about that, Wolf,' she said.

'Don't you have a husband, then?'

'No.' She wiped a strand of hair out of his face with the back of her hand.

'You married him because he's really rich but now you must never let him in again because now you've got money.'

One side of the bean tent had come loose. She pushed the plastic back under the ground and tapped the earth flat, spending a long time on it, her eyelids lowered.

Then he grabbed her, his forehead against her throat, his arms around her shoulders, every part of his body burrowing like the animal that had crawled up out of the ground and was now trying to bury itself under her skin, trying to hide inside her.

'Ssshhh,' she said.

His body was still trembling when she carried him into the house.

'Just go on playing upstairs, boys,' he heard her say. And then again: 'Ssshhh.'

He didn't care whether they were at the top of the stairs, Roman and Andreas, everyone they'd tell at school tomorrow, his mother who would soon peel him away from Tatiana, furious, and his father who would cautiously bring up the subject. He didn't care. She took off her cap and a tent of blonde hair spread itself over him protectively. He trembled and wanted to tremble, as if he were a bean just starting to grow, as if everything that lived in the earth were now lodged inside him, her hair wet with his snot, his tears smeared across her throat, the grip of his hands in the fabric of her T-shirt.

'Ssshhh.'

'Don't slam the door like that, Inge!' shouted his father.

At the age of thirty-two, while attending an archaeological congress, Wolf will find himself enchanted by a researcher from Minsk.

'I don't know what that woman's up to with our son, but he seems ripe for a psychiatrist,' his mother shouted.

After a superficial conversation he'll never see the researcher again and gradually he'll think about her less and less.

'Wolf, just open the door now,' his father said, sounding serious.

When people ask him about it in his old age, he'll describe life as strange and himself as content. But not yet. Now the world is a bedroom no one's allowed into, a handkerchief full of hard, dry flowers, which already stink a bit.

Indeed

It was good that it had been pointed out to Kenneth Selle-slaghs the day before that recycling centres bring peace to the brain. Now he could feel it too. Around the almost empty containers a lazy resignation prevailed of 'keep it coming' and 'there's still room for more'. At the full containers there was the tired but satisfied sort of peace that descended after something had been achieved. And that was despite the fact that in the first two months of his working life he'd found it so noisy here, and unsafe.

'Clearing up,' the little round gypsy woman had summarized in broken Dutch, 'creates peace.' She explained that she should know, because she was a cleaner, which meant she did exactly what he did, only on a smaller scale. 'Never underestimate your job,' she said. 'You have more in your power than you think.' Then she stepped away from him backwards, chuckling mysteriously. When she reached the container of rubble, she got into her Fiat Panda and drove off.

Kenneth stared for a long time at the container of prunings. He'd helped the woman throw two parched olive trees into it and now he climbed up the four rungs of the ladder on the container flank to take another look at them. The little trees lay with their crowns intertwined amid all the amputated branches. Mass grave—he'd overheard that term here once, and in the case of the prunings it made sense. He went back down the ladder, walked past the clear plastic bags of polystyrene to the table with empty paint tins, and stopped beside the strip lights. Probably born in the same factory, they'd now found each other again after a long, lonely journey. That was no doubt the kind of peace the woman had meant.

The notion of peace in his head occupied Kenneth's thoughts until lunchtime.

During the lunch break he ate his sandwiches sitting with his colleagues Ludwig and André. They had a hut to eat in. It wasn't often they could sit in there together undisturbed. Not one car had driven into the recycling centre for the past half-hour.

'Take your time. It isn't healthy, bolting your food like that,' said Ludwig. André was the oldest, but only Ludwig was solicitous, like an older brother, sometimes to the point of kindness.

'Eating fast he can do, working fast is a different matter,' said André. 'When you see him doing something you wonder what's going on in his head. Today he must have stared at those prunings for half an hour, then walked around for a bit. I dare say everyone has to be given a chance, but we do need ...'

'He's here, André. Don't talk about him as if he's not here.'

'I'm here,' Kenneth concurred serenely.

'Do you like working here?' asked Ludwig.

Kenneth nodded. 'Clearing up creates peace in my head.'

The men looked at each other, amused, then simultaneously started laughing. 'So there is something inside there, then?' asked André. He made a fist and tapped Kenneth on the forehead with his knuckles. The sound he made as he did so was supposed to suggest an empty container, Kenneth knew that. André used a lot of sounds to add weight to his words. 'Engine', 'checkout' and 'empty container' were regulars.

'Creates, wow, it "creates" peace, you say. Clever.' Ludwig had cheered right up. So some good had come of it. But this was still teasing.

They thought he was stupid. Everyone thought he was stupid. There had been tests and remedial teachers, and now there were work colleagues nevertheless. They'd all been right. The odd thing was that Kenneth only felt stupid when he was reminded of it. Actually it was like that with everything. Every time a suggestion was made that concerned him, every time he inspired a response, Kenneth imagined sawing open the top of his skull, then lying on his stomach next to the opening and putting his arm down inside, right up to the shoulder. He always fished out something to corroborate the assertion. It was all in there. Could you be stupid if you were so full? Apparently you could.

'Hey, finish your lunch!' Ludwig said when Kenneth stood up. 'Are you angry?'

Kenneth walked over to the scrap metal. Arms raised above his head, he pulled as hard as he could at the tarpaulin, trying to stretch it over the full container.

'Leave that tarp alone, it'll tear!' André turned his attention to his sandwich. He was starting to gobble now too. Sometimes he couldn't stand it any longer.

'All right. Get over there.' Ludwig was suddenly right next to him. Kenneth did as he was told. Together they pulled the tarp over the container, as if they'd gathered up the remains of a steel elephant and were now covering it, ready for burial. A motionless metal elephant, and a moving train. Perhaps the train would come off best, thought Kenneth.

'Stop fretting. And frowning. You have to be able to take a joke. That goes for everyone.'

Actually it was more likely to bring about a derailment, thought Kenneth.

'What you need is a pub crawl,' said Ludwig.

Kenneth looked up at him. A pub crawl. Indeed.

Ludwig was the first to go inside, immediately followed by Kenneth, who held the door open for the whole volleyball team and all the women who'd come with the volleyball players. The team, of which Ludwig was captain, went on a pub crawl every year in a city the members didn't know very well. This season they'd finished near the top of the league table, so the club paid for the first drink in each pub and everyone was allowed to invite someone else.

'It never occurred to me that our boys would bring their wives,' said Ludwig. 'I'm pretty sure there won't be any women, I said to mine. And now here I am, lumbered with you.'

Ludwig laughed, so Kenneth laughed with him. Difficult, he found it, humour.

'What are you drinking?'

'Coke,' he said.

'No,' said Ludwig. 'Not Coke. I'm driving, you're drinking.'

'Beer?'

'I would think so, yes.'

While Ludwig took all the other orders, Kenneth looked around, at the smooth jets pouring out of the beer taps and the ceiling with clouds painted on it. He didn't often go to a pub. The point of it wasn't completely clear to him. The rest of the gathering seemed to know; the volleyball players and their wives were all talking at once, he couldn't understand what they were saying, everything melted together into noise.

'A pleasure,' said the man next to him.

'Not really,' said Kenneth. 'It's a bit cramped in here.'

He just caught sight of the man's hand, which had been about to shake his own, as it withdrew. When Kenneth looked up again, a woman was standing next to the man, wearing a funny hat.

'This is Laura,' the man said. 'And I'm Gerrit.'

Kenneth nodded, wondering what was expected of him.

'And who are you?' said Laura.

'Kenneth Selleslaghs.'

'Are you Ludwig's friend?' Laura wanted to know. 'I mean *the* friend?'

Kenneth hesitantly shook his head.

'Do you play volleyball too?' she asked.

'No, you walk,' said Gerrit. He brought his index finger up close to Kenneth's right nostril. 'With a hiking club? Isn't it?'

Kenneth felt uncertain for a moment because Gerrit had said it with such conviction. He did walk sometimes of course. Perhaps there was even a keen walker hidden inside him. All the same, he shook his head a second time.

'I've had cancer,' said Laura. 'But I'm cured now. Peace is slowly returning.'

'Great!' They smiled at each other.

'Never thought of joining a hiking club?' Gerrit asked.

Before he could come up with an answer, Ludwig announced it was time to move on to the next pub and Kenneth, hemmed in by the volleyball team, was swept out onto the pavement.

In pub after pub, the couple managed to find him. Kenneth talked with Laura about her vanished cancer and with Gerrit about the joys of walking. He did his best to follow both narratives, which wasn't easy as they were mixed together. He understood the frightening moments before an operation and the overwhelming beauty of nature as you walked. Now and then he managed to think of a question that would work for both of them. 'Did it change your life?' was right on the button, for example; in both cases the difference between before and after turned out to be huge.

The noise increased.

'Shall we dance?' Laura asked.

The question took him by surprise. He liked dancing, but he rarely did it with anyone else. He waited helplessly for Gerrit's reaction.

'Go ahead,' said Gerrit. He couldn't have sounded friendlier. 'I don't dance. I'm more one for moving forward step by step in a straight line.'

Kenneth wasn't troubled by the fact that they were the only dancers. He was good at this. It had been said of him many times, and now Laura thought so too. He turned her on her axis and around his own, managing to find her hands again blind, behind his back and above their heads. Gerrit and Ludwig were standing talking, perhaps about him. Gerrit looked distrustful, but he was probably simply preoccupied; Kenneth often got different states of mind mixed up when reading faces.

'Did you notice I don't have any eyebrows?' asked Laura. 'No eyelashes either.' She blinked her eyes exaggeratedly.

He couldn't really tell properly under the red and yellow spotlights. If he liked he could touch the bulge where hair used to be. It would soon grow back, because she was cured; life smiled on her more brightly now than before. It invited change, complete and outright.

Kenneth had just finished running two inquisitive fingers along the hairless eyebrow when Gerrit stepped into his field of vision, coming at him in a straight line, elbow bent and fist balled.

From the ground Kenneth looked up at him. He was amazed he was still conscious, in fact he felt more awake than usual.

'That garbage man has damn well been chatting up my girlfriend ever since the first pub!' Gerrit shouted above everyone as his thrashing body was dragged off by two broad volleyball players. Laura went after them, crying, shouting that she wanted to live with a capital L.

Ludwig helped Kenneth to his feet. He stuffed two corners of his own handkerchief into Kenneth's nose to stop the bleeding. 'Oh, Kenneth,' he said, drunk but in earnest. 'Floored by love.'

Kenneth hadn't seen it that way until now. Probably he hadn't been listening to Laura out of politeness, hadn't been dancing with her purely because he liked dancing. There was sure to have been more to it than that, and his last chance was disappearing out through a pub door in tears. He had to go after her. He too was cured. Walking didn't interest him one bit. 'You have more power than you think,' the gypsy woman had said.

'Whatever you do, stay here,' said Ludwig. Kenneth stopped trying to get to the door. Ludwig squeezed past him, rather unsteadily.

What the rest of the volleyball team and their wives had witnessed through the windows remained hidden from Kenneth. When they all stormed outside in a frenzy, he followed.

Ludwig, having only just been picked up off the street, shouted after Gerrit that he'd be expelled from the club. The four-wheel-drive tore off noisily.

'I love you, Laura!' Kenneth shouted in turn. Whether she'd heard him, he didn't know. Gerrit certainly had. He slammed on the brakes and reversed all the way back to the pub. The volleyball team pushed Kenneth inside, and one man posted himself protectively at the entrance.

'Bring it on!' he heard Ludwig shout.

Kenneth wanted to go home. He reluctantly allowed himself to be dragged to one last pub. The gathering was restless, still worked up by all the pushing and pulling involved in preventing a second fight. They'd all thought this would happen at some point; there had always been something antisocial about Gerrit, hostile even. He was a split personality, incapable of making choices. In any case, walking was a more appropriate occupation for an individualist like him, they believed.

Although Ludwig had taken quite a beating in the first fight—his upper lip wouldn't stop bleeding—he'd persisted in provoking Gerrit. Now he put that same recklessness into the words 'I can always drive!'

'Kenneth,' said the most sober and sensible of the team. 'Ludwig is in no fit state. You'll have to drive.'

'I don't have a driving licence.'

'I thought not.' The volleyball player suddenly sounded irritated. 'Then sit with him and wait till he sobers up. Whatever you do, make sure he doesn't get behind the wheel in that state.'

Kenneth had never imagined Ludwig would be so heavy. He'd thrown his workmate's arm over his shoulders and with great difficulty was steering him towards the car. After protesting loudly, Ludwig had fallen asleep. Halfway there his limp body dragged Kenneth's to the ground with it. When they got to the car, Kenneth propped him carefully against the bodywork, so that his hands were free to search his pockets for the key. Ludwig awoke with a start.

'Police! Police!' he shouted.

Kenneth opened the door and helped him into the passenger seat. There a melancholy haze rose before Ludwig's eyes. Kenneth hurried over to the other side of the car, sat at the wheel and shut the doors from the inside.

'I'm so embarrassed,' said Ludwig in a ghostly voice. 'Take me home.'

'I can't drive,' said Kenneth. 'I don't have a driving licence. I'll stay with you till you're sober.'

'Of course you can drive, Kenneth. Anything's possible if you try hard enough, for God's sake! Don't torment yourself with uncertainty like this. Anyone can drive! Put the key in the ignition, foot on the accelerator and turn the wheel. What's so difficult about that? Just do it!'

The torrent of words had exhausted Ludwig. He burst into profound sobs, and then he was dead to the world.

'Just do it,' thought Kenneth. He put the key in the ignition and glanced at Ludwig: an oversized bird with a battered, wide-open beak expecting a regurgitated worm. If I try hard enough, thought Kenneth, then I can. He started the engine and sought the right pedal. With a growl the car shot out of the parking place, but in the middle of the street it started to jolt, to the accompaniment of a salad-spinner noise that seemed to be coming from the floor. Before Kenneth could discover what it might be, he was back up to speed. I'm a bullet, he thought, not without mortal terror. The wheel turned far more easily than he'd expected. In a wide arc, he drove into the front wall of a house. His head travelled in a wavelike motion in the direction of the windscreen. Ludwig opened his eyes. A few centimetres short of the breaking glass, their heads were thrown backwards again. The airbags had refused to inflate.

A silence prevailed that was broken only by the sound of the salad-spinner, and even that had grown far more distant.

'You all right?' he asked Ludwig, who hadn't even blinked.

'Did I ask you to drive?'

Kenneth wasn't entirely sure whether Ludwig really meant that as a question. He nodded cautiously.

'Out,' said Ludwig.

'Sorry?'

'Get out of here immediately!'

When Ludwig started pushing him, Kenneth understood that he wasn't supposed to drive off as quickly as possible but to get away from the car. He tore himself loose and struggled out, running from the residents of the house, who were standing on the street in their dressing gowns, hands on hips, watching him go, too dumbfounded to give chase. A moving trail of lighted windows ran along the row of houses, curtains were pulled aside, looks cast. He hoped people wouldn't start shouting out what they thought of him. Peace, thought Kenneth. Peace.

Confused and chilled, he waited next to a row of shopping trolleys for it to get light. He had sat down next to them, but the winter had pushed him up off the tiles with frozen hands. A lot of things passed through his mind, but they didn't include a plan or a solution. Going home didn't seem like a good idea. The police were sure to be waiting for him there, or Ludwig, who would no doubt see to it that he lost his job. Strange, Kenneth thought: the turn his life had taken in a brief span of time was as dramatic as that of the car on its way to the wall. He racked his brain to discover how he might have avoided what had gone wrong but he couldn't work it out.

If only the woman with the olive trees would come round again, he thought. She'd be able to explain to him how he should go about it, creating space, how it could lead him to a way out.

He decided to wait until the supermarket opened. Then he

would take a trolley and push it around until he saw some-one like the gypsy woman, someone who looked nice, and walk with them to a car boot, a garage or a front door. With any luck they'd instruct him on what he needed to do, tell him what kind of a person he was.

It got light. Kenneth looked for the rising sun but gave up when he realized it might be a long time before it came into view from behind the blocks of flats. A good while before opening time, a number of people gathered as close as pos-sible to the supermarket entrance. None of them looked nice enough. The checkout girls who arrived after a short while walked through the little group as if it wasn't there. With sleepy arrogance, they did take stock of Kenneth. Inside they turned on the lights.

Kenneth didn't join the people by the entrance, who were now being allowed in. He would take a trolley only when somebody showed up who tempted him to.

He looked at the shoppers clambering out of their cars or off their bicycles. Many unreadable faces. The few words he caught were severe or prickly. 'That's all because of you! It's all your fault!' one of the women shouted at a crying infant that was nevertheless trying to press itself against her broad thigh.

Kenneth was so daunted by the scene that he didn't at first notice the plump teenager standing in front of him. When he did look at her he was immediately overwhelmed by an avalanche of understanding and empathy.

'Give me your hand.' It was almost a whisper.

Kenneth held out his hand. She wanted to put something into it; he hoped it wasn't an insect.

A one-euro coin lay in his palm. Did she think he didn't have money for a shopping trolley?

'You can't help it. You haven't chosen this life,' she said.

That was true enough. All the same, Kenneth realized now that there had been a misunderstanding.

'I'm not begging here,' he said, though he immediately wondered whether that was the case.

She pursed her lips a little, blinked slowly, negated his statement with endless patience.

My goodness, thought Kenneth, I'm leading the life of a tramp.

'Can I offer you a warm meal?' she asked. 'Soup?'

Before long he was walking beside her, past the food. She asked him what his favourite vegetables were and he placed them on the scale. Every time he put an item into the trolley, he insisted he would pay for it himself. She didn't respond to that.

The house she enticed him into smelled of cleaning fluids, essential oils and flowers. The scents were so dominant they made Kenneth's empty stomach contract. He eyed the sofa and would have loved to stretch out on the soft cushions, pull a blanket over him and shut his tired eyes.

The girl invited him to sit at the kitchen table and started rapidly cutting vegetables with a large knife, like a Japanese chef in a cookery competition. She rinsed the pieces and threw them into a bowl of water along with two stock cubes.

'We used to have seven cats,' she said without turning towards him. 'But they all died. All inside of two months. All of the same illness.'

'Oh,' said Kenneth.

The girl began vigorously seasoning the soup.

'It's an induction hob,' she said. 'It's very quick.'

Then she came to sit facing him. For the first time she had nothing to do and Kenneth could see it was making her nervous. She wasn't the right age to be cooking soup. He imagined a flood and someone looking up at the girl from a lifeboat, then sailing away without her. She would watch the boat from the first-floor window, with the same expression as she had now. Kenneth was determined to eat everything she put in front of him, just to make her happy.

'You can't stay the night here,' she said. 'I promised my mother and her boyfriend. That no one would stay the night here, I mean. They wouldn't know, because they're travelling, but trustworthiness is something I value very highly.'

Kenneth nodded.

'You can have a nap on the sofa after you've eaten, though,' she said. 'That's not staying the night.'

Again Kenneth nodded, more gratefully this time.

They waited until the induction hob had done its work. The girl turned on the radio to soak up the silence.

'Nothing to write home about,' said someone in the studio. 'But tolerable.'

'You're right,' the woman hosting the show laughed.

Next came a jittery number that Kenneth made no attempt to understand. He swallowed the first spoonful of hot soup and said it tasted good. A fountain of pepper blasted his nose.

'Thank you,' said the girl.

Some thirty spoonfuls later he thanked her and asked

whether it really was all right to lie down on the sofa for a bit. It was.

He couldn't remember a single dream afterwards, only that he'd driven into the wall again. It had woken him up.

The girl was pulling wilted petals from an arrangement of flowers. When she noticed he was awake she came to stand next to the sofa and looked down at him with her head to one side.

'You look rested!' she exclaimed. 'Even happy! There's so much more you can achieve!'

She spread her arms out in front of her at the end of every sentence. There was a maniac hidden inside her, Kenneth realized now, but she was right. The sun smeared thick layers of honey on the windows. Outside everything was being prepared.

The Party

Animals outside. Tractors, awnings and yet more animals. A house of glass, what's it called? Ordinary houses and gardens, houses, a garden with a swimming pool—swimming! Conservatory! That's what it's called: conservatory. Grass. Grass. Grass. Clouds. Grass. Grass. Grass. Grass. Grass. A child, a child that you know, because it waves at you and you wave back, you stand up and want to run through the train, 'go back, go back', a clearly repeated command from the tracks, back, back, back, past the windows, to look at the child that you know.

There's a hand on the sleeve of your thin shirt, a beautiful hand with elegant, smooth fingers and manicured nails, gently pushing you downwards, wanting you to sit. You sit down. You follow the arm, from where the hand belongs up to the shoulder, the friendly face of a young lady, sunlight glowing through, sometimes disappearing but always returning as trembling lozenge-shaped facets, stripes, rays. What a treasure, what a sweet, light treasure.

'Sweetheart,' you say, laughing at the crazy word. You taste the sugary word: 'sweetheart'.

She laughs too, the way water laughs, and her round cheeks move, her little teeth gleam, a dimple appears on each side of her smile. You stretch out your old hand and dip your index finger in one, very cautiously, and again. She folds up your fingers with her own and presses her tender cheek to them. She closes her eyes, as if about to fall asleep; you sit there motionless, and then she looks up after all and gazes at you, not letting you go; you don't know what you've done to deserve her, but she makes you fragile and blissful and you don't want to see it, you don't want to see the worry that shows through in that look, the hidden sadness that you know from others, even though you don't know which others, perhaps you're imagining it, the sadness, the others— she's smiling, isn't she? The cheeks, the dimples.

'We're nearly there,' she says.

You nod.

She turns her face to the glass, her eyes darting this way and that, jerkily. You want her to stop it, it's making you nervous. It's better that she looks at you, doesn't take her eyes off you, you're waiting for that but it doesn't come, so you look at the trees and the grass, then houses again, more and more houses, no grass any longer, few trees. One of those Baltic states, you think and then you ask, after all: 'Where are we nearly?'

'At the party, Dominique,' she says. 'We're going to a party.'

Dominique. So that's your name.

The building is high, the floor far too full. Someone bumps into you without looking round, without making excuses. You want to sit on the ground but she stops you and pulls you upright. People are looking.

'The station is busy,' she says. 'It'll be better outside. Give me your arm,' and while the two of you walk locked together like a conjurer's rings, you know what you've been, what you could still be: a gentleman. You straighten your back and touch the crown of your head. Unfortunately you're not wearing a hat.

Dignified, you step out together into the sun-drenched city. Here too people are staring, but no one walks into you. Cars stop at zebra crossings. You politely greet the drivers as you cross. They look straight through you at her bare legs and you can't really blame them, she looks great in her blue dress, with the sun blasting fire into her long brown hair. Her earrings are tiny pearls and they prance along with each step you take, with the heartbeat in your throat.

'What are you looking at?' she asks.

You point to the pearls and she shakes her head to make them move in all directions. You hope she's your wife; she's all you could wish for. Desire gives way to shyness. You can't recall any children, any fatherhood, but you do know a few of the rules of the world you're wandering in, and one of them is that not remembering something doesn't necessarily mean that it never existed, that it never happened. This woman could be your granddaughter. She probably is your granddaughter. Having such a beautiful granddaughter fills you with pride. But you still hope she's your wife.

'How exactly are things between us?' you ask airily. 'You and me, what do you think about it yourself?'

'What I think?' she asks—you've got her smiling again; that's nice. 'I think I'll take good care of you, look after you properly, that's what I think.'

'How long have we known each other now?'

'I've had this job for two years.'

You stop, overcome by dizziness and gravity. She's paid to be with you. How can she think that's acceptable? She folds her arms and frowns patiently.

'Who pays you?'

'Your cousin.'

Cousin. The word evokes nothing. You wait, incomprehensible flashes follow, then a story in four images: an electric fence around a meadow, your hand that absorbs the pain but doesn't let go of the wire, a boy—cousin?—who takes you by the shoulders and shouts and swears and shares your pain, the disbelief as you look at each other. Cousin.

There is suddenly a great deal that distances you from her, a great deal you don't dare ask her, but she understands she needs to introduce herself now.

'I trained as a nurse,' she says. 'But I don't want to work in a hospital any longer, I only want to care for you, so stop grouching and stay alive as long as you can. I need you.'

There she is again with her little teeth and the love that dances about on her face.

'What's your name?' you ask.

'Emmy,' she says, and then: 'Starlings!' Delighted, she points to the sky.

A huge monster is gliding over the rooftops. It grows and shrinks from grey to black, changes direction unexpectedly, becomes a snake, becomes a hook, becomes a head that jerks round to face you.

'It's breathing!' you shout. People look. They're unaware that their end is nigh.

'Don't be afraid.'

You let her stroke your back and try to believe what she

says. That it's hundreds of silly birds and they can't do anything to you, not even collectively. That they're only out to show you their tricks, like everyone else.

'Come on,' she says, making her arm into a loop again, an invitation you're glad to accept, and you walk on like that, close together. You don't look back, don't look at the sky.

'They're expecting us,' says Emmy.

They. The questions tire you.

Us. That's clear.

They all seem to like you. Emmy has just steered you into a room full of books and people when applause breaks out that scares you stiff, but you bow. It's automatic, the bowing and the blowing of kisses, princely and practised in equal measure. You notice that Emmy is astonished by it and you slowly shrug at her. Go ahead, she says with her lips, so you go ahead, you've no need to feel embarrassed.

You're slapped on the back and addressed by name, Dominique here, Dominique there; that's enough, you think, I know it now.

Two men start squabbling over what they call 'your work', about themes and periods and critics, sales figures and art and behind them a boy walks past with a tray of tiny crackers with salmon and pâté and sushi with egg and avocado.

'Here!' you call out.

The men laugh and one of them asks if you're hungry, but you see what happens to their faces when you pile up the food in your hand, in your mouth. It's not polite, you realize, not gentlemanly, but who knows how long you'll have to wait for a fresh tray. Chewing, you go over to stand next to Emmy.

'This is William,' she says. 'The cousin we were talking about just now.'

You have no idea what she means and you shake the red-haired man's red-haired hand. He looks nice, not a kisser. Then you notice it in him too, that holding back, that mournful curiosity, so you walk away from him. Emmy doesn't follow but continues talking to him, which unsettles you.

You look at the books on the shelves on the walls, on the tables, at the photos and drawings with their colours, some with hard covers, some soft—those are the best ones, you can make wind with those. You try it, holding a book near your face and letting the pages slip past your thumb very fast. The wind makes the tiny hairs on your ears move, an exceptionally pleasant sensation, so you carry on doing it for a while. You try to ignore the fact that you're hemmed in by a semicircle of people, but a woman steps up to you. She would take the book out of your hand if you weren't holding it so firmly and she says: 'Yes, that's the one thing it's good for. As long as you're not going to read it, it's trash.'

You laugh the way that you laugh along with everything here. You don't read anything. You have distant visions of books in your lap, in bed, in trains, they were friends of yours, in a long other life, and, just as you loved certain people, you loved books, you spent a lot of time with them, you know that, but you can't detect any pattern in the symbols on the pages, collections of dead fruit flies, that's what books are, and people are made of eyes and noise. Where is Emmy?

'Dominique Favarque,' says a man with a ghastly appearance, expectation in his voice. He doesn't join in your laughter.

'Is there really no trace of me left in there?' He tickles his brow.

You try to look over the tops of people's heads. Surely Emmy can't have gone?

'Leave that bearded woman alone for a bit,' says the man and you try to consider what he means but he distracts you, shoves an open book under your nose and a pen into your hand.

'For Alex,' he says.

You want to be outside, to feel the wind.

'Here,' he says, and he points at the white surface. 'For Alex, my biographer.'

You put the tip of the pen down, press it into the paper, take it away again. The result interests you: a minuscule black pit. You search for the right distance above the page to be able to study it; with your nose too close you can't see it any more.

When you look up at the man, something occurs to you, something you recall about people: malice. It must have been there a lot and now it's here.

You spin round and find yourself eye to eye with Emmy. 'I need a loo,' you say.

She wrenches the pen out of your hand and gives it back to the man rather brusquely. 'Come with me,' she says.

Although you now urgently need to go to the toilet, the doors remain locked. Behind those doors, women are talking nonsense.

'Dominique does look happy, though.'

'So old.'

'So thin.'

'Let's hope it never happens to us.'

'You going to be much longer?' you call out. 'I desperately need to pee!'

On the other side of the doors there is silence.

'A little lipstick?' Emmy asks.

She looks at you through a window. Next to her is a short-haired woman. She's wearing a blue shirt and black trousers and she's watching you attentively. She seems to want to recall who you are, which puts you at ease. At exactly the same moment you nod to each other. Behind her a door opens, then another. Two people hurry off, but you don't look at them, because you can't tear yourself away from the woman.

'Lipstick?' asks Emmy, who is now standing next to you and next to the woman as well, who does what you do but seems to think it's you who's copying her, she looks so angry.

'Have I upset her?' you ask Emmy. You point at the woman, who points back.

'That's you, Dominique.'

'I'm Dominique,' you say, again at the same time as the woman, who seems no less sincere about it than you. 'I'm a gentleman?'

'No, my love,' Emmy moans. 'That's a mirror. That's us.'

There are indeed two Emmys. You decide to believe them. You're that woman there.

'A mirror,' Emmy says again.

Dominique nods at you hesitantly. You smile at her and

152

she smiles back. You're both a good bit younger than you imagined.

'You probably dreamed last night that you were a man,' says Emmy.

You shake your head. You don't blame her and don't explain. Emmy can't know that there's no such thing as dreaming.

'I'm not a man either, by the way,' she says. 'In case you think I am, with this beard.'

Beard?

'Put on a bit of lipstick then,' you say, turning to Emmy and pouting.

'Lips taut.' She shows you how and places the greasy tip on your bottom lip. Unpleasant, you think. Not something to be repeated.

'Done,' says Emmy.

The mouth of Dominique in the mirror looks far bigger now.

Emmy prints a red kiss on the back of your hand with her mouth and you do the same on hers.

'Look,' says Emmy, again surrounded by people. Leave that book where it is, you think. Leave all the books where they are and pretend they don't exist, but she's already turned it over and she's showing you the photo on the back flap.

It's the woman in the window, you. So that was Dominique, the way she used to be, maybe not even so long ago, when she sat at a table with a feeble smile for a photo on a book cover.

'You wrote this,' says Emmy softly. 'You've written many books. This is your party.'

The tears well up very quickly, fall very quickly into your lap. It doesn't matter what Emmy says—until she says you can leave, if that's what you want.

You nod. She briefly strokes your ear.

Then the hugging starts, an endless succession of arms that clasp you, tummies that are squeezed up against you and, although you don't like the sticky kisses on your skin and the incomprehensible words they throw in your face with tiny drops of spit, you persist in smiling, you smile at every sound they emit; this is what they want, this is how you survive them and you don't know why but you think: hundreds of silly birds.

Close By

This was actually Lady LaToya's first trip. True, she'd done the stretch from Sao Paulo to Pattaya, but she'd never been Lady LaToya uninterruptedly over there. When she flew to those destinations she was Kurt, in a nondescript T-shirt and light linen trousers. With Kurt everything was just fine. He knew what was going on in Lady LaToya's heart, so he'd been generous enough to give her two of his three weeks' holiday. Lady LaToya was in need of it.

Her colleagues had advised her against travelling as La-Toya. They warned her of problematic passport checks and repressive cultures, of attackers, even the possibility of castration. A dressing room full of those solicitous advisers had sniggered at the remark by one of them—Missy May, who else?—that she shouldn't put herself through it, all that walking, up and down stairs, in and out of aircraft, that at least she ought to look for a pair of comfortable sandals, something orthopaedic, flip-flops if need be. LaToya answered that anyone can break a heel, that it was just bad luck if it happened during a show. Missy May whispered 'no hysteria, darling', her attention already back on her eyelashes in the mirror. Get right away, LaToya had decided on the spot.

So now she was in a train to the airport, pretending not to notice that the couple in the seat across the aisle were giving her sour looks. They hadn't realized they could slide their luggage between the backs of two seats and had squeezed their white, varicose-veined legs around suitcases that were no less impractical than they were unfashionable. That kind of moronic disapproval and inept ugliness had at one time put Lady LaToya to flight. A new, feather-light world had spread itself out at her feet, and she'd dived into it without a second thought, with a graceful somersault.

In an attempt to come across as young in spirit, some of her contemporaries claimed these days that their home port had always had its downside. Not true. It used to be great and now it was rotten. These past fifteen years it had all been increasingly professionalized and sponsored, celebrated and isolated, pumped up and sucked dry. Never before had so many queens joined in. Public interest was growing as well. Anyone following that little world less closely than LaToya might have concluded it had grown more animated, fuller, but she knew the most important thing of all had gone, leaving behind it a gaping hole: pleasure.

The rivalry and venom that the new guard of princely witches brought with them had been giving LaToya gastritis and migraine attacks for far too long already. She was seriously considering retiring for good, calling a halt to her performances. According to Kurt she had reached an age for that. Although she was sometimes mistaken for fifteen years younger, she was well past fifty, only two years short of sixty in fact. But where was she supposed to shine then, where could she exist? A definitive parting struck fear into Kurt as well. He didn't want to risk his inner harmony, to which Lady LaToya had made an essential contribution, by losing her. A future as a travelling transvestite was not something LaToya aspired to; she'd no desire to show herself to all and sundry. She was now on her way in Kurt's place to a quiet island in the Dodecanese, because that was what she needed, to have a good think, to bring something to a close, perhaps. If this first journey also proved her last, she mustn't regard that as a failure. It was an eventuality certain to reveal itself as the start of something new.

She tossed back the smooth hair of her wig and slid both index fingers under the shoulder straps of her summer dress.

First the journey itself, she thought. You often heard it said that it was ultimately all about that, the path, the journey. And she'd only just left.

Lady LaToya put her mother-of-pearl Cosmolite on the scales. She'd had to save up for the largest size of the shell-inspired suitcase, and contrary to her intentions she'd bought a matching beauty case too. But it had been worth it; she'd rarely seen Missy May so envious. Fortunately the beauty case was made of indestructible material. It unnerved her to watch the two pieces of luggage sail away from the check-in desk. She responded with magnanimity to the scornful look the airport official cast at Kurt's photo. 'Shall I take off my hair?' she offered.

There was no need for that.

Hidden camera, thought Lady LaToya when she saw the angel standing at the gate. But the sublime twenty-something wasn't play-acting, or at any rate not in a role invented by others. His combed-back hair framed the face of a mysterious prince from an exotic fairy tale, possibly a genie. His clothes were pure white, his wings white and heavy, his back very straight, a dancer.

When he raised his eyes to look at her, LaToya felt soft caresses to her steaming back, her Adam's apple, her outsized feet, the compressed fat under the corset. This wasn't the idea, she thought.

She'd gone to sit on a seat with her back to him, but when she joined the queue for the final passport check she felt him standing behind her, close by. Through the glass wall in front of the jetway she saw him inflamed by an argument. His passport wasn't handed back and he was asked to stand to one side, which he did, annoyed. Under white fabric his buttocks tightened. She carried on walking.

The seat next to hers was occupied by a woman in a tracksuit who had already fallen asleep, although she couldn't have sat down more than a minute or two before LaToya. Her open mouth offered a captivating tour of the advances in dentistry of recent decades.

A stewardess with her hair in a messy bun and lipstick on her chin strode obliquely along the gangway with the angel's wings in her arms. In surly Greek she said something to a steward, who seemed to panic but then took the wings from her all the same. LaToya watched him go, but she couldn't see what he did with them. Nor could she spot the wingless angel.

She pulled her handbag out from under the seat in front, rummaged in it and looked at herself in a pocket mirror. The colours on her eyelids and lips hadn't smudged; everything was still inside the lines. With a brush and some powder she eliminated the shine on her cheeks and brow. She knew of no one else who commanded the art of make-up like she did. She was a person who was good at something, who was good at a great many things, loudmouthed Lady LaToya. The self-confidence that had deserted her under the angel's gaze was coming back.

A stewardess, not the one who had carried off the wings, bent down over her unexpectedly, and slightly flirtatiously.

'There's an empty seat next to your friend,' she said. 'If you want.'

'What do you mean?' LaToya didn't need to look to see where she was pointing. She couldn't understand why she'd failed to notice the back of his head until now.

'You don't …? I thought … I'm so sorry.'

'We don't,' she smiled and she added maternally: 'No problem.' The stewardess had gone red.

LaToya had always thought happiness lay in being able to seize opportunities. What was she trying to avoid?

Coming here was a great idea, she thought as she stepped into the bath of hot air. Here the light made people more beautiful. The sequins on LaToya's dress flashed with every step of her stilettos.

On one of the two luggage belts in the small airport a long procession of suitcases was led by her Cosmolite. In a single, fluid movement she picked up the cases and pulled them along the floor behind her. Life suggested that it was good.

She saw herself on a map, the taxi ride she would soon be taking, a dotted line to the seaside resort where a boat would moor to carry her across a strip of sea to a smaller, lesser-known island. One with a volcano.

'Kardamaina,' she said to the taxi driver as he was putting the Cosmolite in the boot. He seemed to see her for the first time and looked her up and down.

'Me too.' A soft male voice. The angel, with his wings on again. A flawless face, dark and Eastern. Perfection. Glow.

The taxi driver nodded and took his bag.

'How much?' asked the angel, who wasn't going to pay any more than necessary, who could think of such things now. He repeated his question in Greek.

'Fifteen,' said the driver. LaToya deduced from his gestures that he was suggesting, in his own language, that the wings should be tossed in the boot. He didn't insist when the offer was declined.

It wasn't comfortable, sitting with wings on. Lopsided, their white feathers pressed against LaToya's shoulder. The angel was leaning forward slightly, almost right on the edge of the back seat.

'Do you speak Dutch?'

He looked round and smiled far more sweetly, far more fondly than she'd expected.

'Sure I do.'

'Didn't they let you keep the wings on in the plane?' It was a silly question to ask. He was aware that she already knew the answer.

'Safety regulations.' He rolled his eyes to the taxi roof. 'Could anything be more ridiculous?'

In different circumstances LaToya would have thought things could always be more ridiculous, but now it did indeed strike her as highly inappropriate and reprehensible that there were regulations about depriving an angel of his wings. She nodded in sympathy.

As the hills and the arid fields passed them, she searched for something to say, hoping he might initiate a conversation.

The silence persisted until they drove into the little town. Kardamaina was hell, LaToya realized when the taxi slowed down. The hotels spewed drunken and debilitated British kids out onto the street. From all directions came the sound of ringtones, mopeds and arguments; here and there a teenage girl in a bikini stood cursing and crying in the sunburned arms of a friend. According to billboards a Big Mac cost only a euro. The lager flowed liberally in bars with no closing time.

Lady LaToya said it out loud: 'A hell.'

The angel grinned.

'Were you planning on staying here?'

'No, thank God!'

They each paid half the fare. LaToya told him the name of the island she was sailing to. It was the angel's destination as well, a fact that seemed to cause the first blue waves she saw to crash right inside her head. He would be there too. All her other thoughts took to treading water.

The boat wasn't sailing. According to the captain the sea was too rough; according to the Brit who served them their calamari it had to do with the crisis.

'We'll find a speedboat somewhere that can take us,' said Lady LaToya to the angel, mainly because she was eager to toss that sentence nonchalantly his way. The prospect made her almost crazy with enthusiasm—racing over the waves with a scarf round her head and sunglasses on, an angel at her side.

'You think so?' the angel asked. He was called Nico Min, had a Greek mother and a Belgian-Korean father, was barely twenty-five and had lived on every continent, not counting the poles. He ate with abandon. Imagine if he'd taken a different flight, or the same flight in different clothes, the same clothes in a different taxi, to a different island, far away from her. But he hadn't, he'd been close at her heels, it had been impossible to avoid him. Now she would have to find a fast boat.

She started each stage of their questioning with a girlish 'kalimera', which seemed to please Nico Min, although he always took over from her in fluent Greek.

An hour and a half later they found a helpful woman who prevailed upon her silent father. Without looking at them, the man accepted the agreed sum and powered the motorboat across the deep blue. He could smoke against the wind.

Lady LaToya tied the ends of her scarf in a double knot under her chin. Behind them hell grew smaller and quieter until it disappeared from sight, leaving only wide water, sky, and Nico Min, who made no attempt to talk over the noise of the engine but smiled at her. All this was for them.

Nico put their luggage on the quayside. After he'd helped her disembark he went on holding her hand and brought his face close to hers. His lips tasted salty, hers probably too.

'What does a young angel want with such an old princess?' She immediately wished she hadn't asked. It had sounded so weary, shy yet flirtatious. Perhaps he didn't want anything.

'You're magnificent,' was his verdict.

He stayed in a different, more expensive hotel and didn't suggest she spend the night with him. Lady LaToya, who walked around the edge of the island to her own room, didn't interpret the absence of the question as an attempt to make her hungry. This wasn't about the build-up she loved so much, that time of expectation when the real beginning could still come to nothing. There was no build-up going on, nor any longing that might yet run aground. They'd shared a boat and a couple of meals, enjoyed the sea, the inertia that had crept into their walks, the sloping streets where sunlight and shade had marked out separate territories, the evening air.

Now they listened in their own beds to the sloshing of the waves between the rocks, ready to slip off into a deep, child-like sleep. She couldn't imagine any better company with which to arrive on a quiet island and she felt grateful for the day that had passed. The kiss had been a kiss of astonishment. On her part as well as his. Tomorrow she would give Nico Min a casual wave, a slow salute, perhaps, should he happen to walk through the heat towards her.

Lady LaToya turned onto her other side.

Nico Min.

Good name.

She shaved under the shower and rinsed the Veet from her legs. The night had been restless, with confused dreams to prove she had actually slept.

By the time she'd put on a pair of knickers and stuffed her bra, drops of sweat were rolling down her forehead again. She was so stingy sometimes. A room with air-conditioning would still have been cheap. Now she needed to try to get a refreshing stream of air flowing between the window and the door to the corridor. She put on a dress and opened both a bit further.

There he was. Sitting on the terrace below the balcony. She could see his back. The weight of the wings, which were leaning against a small table, had left a wet imprint on his yellow T-shirt. An angel on vacation. He was drinking Fanta and waiting.

Lady LaToya tried not to hurry, tried not to sweat. Make-up required patience. The wig was intolerable, making the foundation pour down to her chin, while the lines of kohl above her eyes wound up angular and asymmetrical. She started again, focusing mainly on her lips, then chose a suitable fuchsia scarf that she wound around her head, as African as possible, donned her sunglasses and strode downstairs.

'Heeey!' she called out, exaggeratedly surprised and as if she'd forgotten his name.

He looked up at her over the frames of his sunglasses.

'It's hot,' he said.

She nodded.

'Can I leave my wings in your room? Just getting here was too much for me with that weight on my back.' He smiled, embarrassed.

'Of course.'

He walked upstairs behind her. Her rattan shoes made a grating noise suggestive of farting. Like a nun she waited in the doorway as he laid his wings on the bed. Madly in love she was. Madly in love and scared to death.

'Where would you like to go?' he asked.

'I've never seen a volcano.'

He seemed to hesitate. Perhaps she was the first person he'd met who had never seen a volcano.

'It's bound to be even hotter there,' he said. 'Can we do that this evening? Let's have a swim now!'

Can we. Let's. Silly boy.

'Give me fifteen minutes,' said Lady LaToya. 'To change into something else.'

He admired her swimsuit but was of the opinion that it had to get wet. They were alone here. Who was holding her back?

'I'll stick to paddling!' LaToya called out for the third time to the head among the waves.

What followed was as predictable as it was exciting. He sang the theme from *Jaws*, disappeared underwater and emerged again close by, then straightened up. She shrieked. She ran as she hadn't run in years but she couldn't prevent him from pulling her off-balance, carrying her as soon as the sea began to help him. After that, slow motion.

'What on earth are you doing, Nico Min?'

'I'm holding you in my arms. I'm breaking down the last of your defences.'

'As long as my head doesn't get wet.'

Lady LaToya stretched out her right leg and drew the outline of the sun with her foot. Her toenails glittered like pink sweets, glistening drips slipped from her beautiful legs to her crotch. Missy May ought to see this, she thought for a moment, but when she imagined Missy May catching sight of Nico Min from the beach she was glad she wouldn't be coming. For me, thought Lady LaToya, for us.

On the beach he told her about himself. He'd always been

rich. A career was optional. He'd felt guilty about that for a long time, although not always to the same degree. He liked dancing, regarding it for a while as a necessity, a passion, and he'd got himself a place at ballet school. Before the first term began, however, he started to imagine what would happen to him if he lived for a dream: the never-ending commitment and urge for perfection, the toll of daily training, the injuries, the eating disorders, the harsh treatment, first from teachers, later from fellow dancers and the media, the seclusion, the settling of scores, then the bitterness. He abandoned the idea and danced now and then in the privacy of his garden.

'I'd say you were born to shine,' said Lady LaToya. 'But it's a fair assessment you've made. They feed on your adversity.'

As he rubbed oil into her back she told him about her career, especially the successes, nothing about a broken heel. She avoided mentioning years. The fact that she was already making a splash with her Tina Turner act fifteen years before Nico Min was born—that mattered. She felt young now, fully alive under his hands, but too old to underestimate the importance of discretion.

The man with long hair and a beard who took them to the volcano claimed he was the only taxi driver on the island. There used to be a woman too, but she'd become ill. Multiple sclerosis. Only forty-eight. He also had a restaurant, called Bambi's, because that was his name: Bambi Papathanassiou.

Nico Min and Lady LaToya chuckled. When Bambi joined in they laughed out loud.

'My nickname,' said Bambi. He shrugged. 'Come and eat.'

They promised not to forget about his restaurant and

asked him to pick them up again in three hours. Bambi insisted they limit their visit to two. It was a small volcano.

'An old Jesus,' said Nico Min as the taxi drove away.

He was my age, thought Lady LaToya. She ran a short distance from him and his sentence, running against the wind, which led a secluded life here between the highest hills on the island. There was a small volcano museum and a café. LaToya looked down over the balustrade. That was it, then, an ochre slope. A family was walking around at the bottom.

'What a charming little volcano,' said Nico Min.

They'd both expected to find boiling lava that you could look at only from a suitable distance. Either that or the carbonized remains of rock, black dust.

'I want to go in!' she called out. 'I want to go in with Nico Min!'

Hand in hand they ran down its flank, with startled, driven legs. Perhaps very few had done it before her on such high heels. She didn't think about falling, so she didn't fall.

The closer they got to the bottom, the more emphatic the smell of sulphur became. Dotted about were holes cordoned off with red-and-white ribbon. Inquisitive, they walked towards one. On the way Nico Min stopped.

'I reckon the ground is glowing.' He bent forward, legs straight, and placed his palms flat on the ground. 'Hot! Just feel it!'

'How supple you are,' said LaToya.

They tried to look into the marked-off hole.

The family caught sight of them and began clambering up the far side of the crater.

'Underfloor heating with lava,' said Nico Min. He looked

at her, aghast. 'Why hasn't anyone ever thought of that?'

She studied his face. He seemed to mean it. Good, she thought, I'm cleverer, so that's my role. She didn't want to trouble him with rectifications just yet.

'I ought to have brought my wings,' he said. 'Inside a volcano with my wings. We could take some fantastic photographs here.'

'We can come back. We're still around.'

It was something they hadn't talked about yet: how long this would last. They went to lie side by side in the warm dust, as if at the bottom of a yellow bucket, gazing at the spotless blue.

'I think I'm in love with you,' said Nico Min. 'I'm in love with you. And what I'm desperate for now is grapes.'

Lady LaToya had to swallow a few times before she managed to say he could have all the grapes he wanted, all he needed to do was exist.

Driving away from the volcano, they promised Bambi they'd eat at his place the following day. LaToya explained they were sticking to fruit that evening. Grapes. Bambi didn't pursue the matter.

The first little shop had only tomatoes and bananas in stock. The shopkeeper seemed upset at being unable to satisfy their desires and referred them on to another islander. LaToya bought two ripe purple bunches. They each ate their way through one in the evening sunlight.

'I want to fetch my wings,' said Nico Min.

'Of course.' LaToya's sparkle persisted while doubt shot through her veins.

In her room he took off his shirt. He carefully lifted the wings from the mattress, hooked them over his shoulders and rested them on the bronzed flesh of his back. Then he closed the door, took her hand from the doorknob and led her to the bed. He gently pushed her backwards. She lay down as if under the dress he was unbuttoning she were made of feathers too. First he hovered protectively above her, smelling of sulphur and sea, then he descended.

In the morning she could barely distinguish between the night and the dream. She recalled a strange, densely populated world of beautiful, languid bodies, a heaving ocean of peachy skin. Muscular arms submerge her, hug her waist, pass her between them. She slowly turns over and over; she seems to be swimming, floating, gravity abolished, space infinite. When she breathes in, desert air fills her lungs, then with a soft moan she breathes out. Her buttocks arouse a warm lap, nipples stroke her back, broad lips encompass her member. She flies, slowly skimming the gyrating bodies, watching Nico Min hovering above them in the lotus position and waving, waving. She's at home here. She's safe here. Kurt is here and she and Nico Min—the others emanate from them. They've been waiting for her, under the command of an angel. They form a bed of big hands that stroke her from hair to shoulders to belly to knees, calves, toes and back again, faster and faster, until they stop and she's on fire. She feels Nico Min swell, wants him inside her, feels her nakedness giving him pleasure. She waits. He makes her wait. His mouth comes down and prints soft kisses on her. For a moment they stay bound together by a silver thread. Then he creeps inside her, first sliding slowly, then jolting. He moans and she feels round behind her, catches hold of his rear, turns over. Their lips and tongues devise the same rhythm, their hands grasp the scruff of each other's neck. Their world is a world of warm mist. Of all conceivable unions, this is theirs.

Nico Min wanted to see the other side of the island. The determination with which he went in search of a means of transport displeased Lady LaToya a little. She'd rather have spent the day on the hot sand or at the bottom of the volcano, lying next to him, bombarded by snippets of the past night.

She wouldn't complain. She would be youthful enough for a moped. If he found a moped more refreshing than a car with all the windows open, then that's how it would have to be. It wasn't exactly unpleasant anyhow to hug his waist tight. She straightened her back and tried to use her leg muscles to absorb the potholes in the road as elegantly as she could.

Nevertheless, her behind felt black and blue after an hour on the road. Her head, too, hot under wig and helmet, seemed numb. Sand stuck to her teeth and her eyes watered. But she had a rider, a knight to hold onto.

The other side of the island turned out to be mostly occupied by a military base. The soldiers standing at the barbed wire watched them with interest when they turned back.

Nico Min drove to the nearest beach. 'This must be the furthest point we can get to,' he said.

They dismounted and briefly kissed. It was markedly cooler here. LaToya had the feeling the wind had come down out of the hills. A turbulent sea stretched away thinly beneath their feet. They pulled off their shoes and followed the new beach. She held his hand and kept looking up at him. It annoyed her that she couldn't think of anything to make him smile. Her yearning for reassurance was so great it was disgusting.

'Did you enjoy last night?' she asked eventually, sounding too vulnerable, almost desperate. She'd danced on tables in a G-string, sailed above jubilant faces in a swing hung with flowers. He ought to have seen it, her past.

He stopped walking and looked at her with some incredulity. 'Yes, of course I did.'

She turned the back of his hand to her mouth and planted a kiss on it.

With his arm over her shoulders, he pulled her close. They walked on like that. Lady LaToya knew she ought to be happy but she thought: is this pity?

They both saw him at the same time. The drowned man. Beyond the rocks the beach curved round and that was where he'd been washed up. They sprinted towards him, fascinated by the sight, by his soaking-wet clothes. When they tried to turn him onto his back he frowned and looked up at them, confused.

'Cut!' It was shouted at them from the distance. Only then did they see the film crew. The drowned man stood up and they all looked at someone with a clipboard under his arm who was striding towards them.

'We're so sorry!' LaToya called out to him frivolously. Nico Min burst out laughing.

'Daniel, stay lying down please,' the man called. 'We'll continue immediately.'

'I feel a little sick,' said the drowned man.

'We'll be off right away,' LaToya soothed.

They briefly expressed their surprise that they all had the Dutch language in common.

'You're a very convincing corpse,' Nico Min said to the drowned man. That wasn't news to him, apparently.

'It's for a television series,' said the man with the clipboard. He coughed nervously. 'Maybe we can have a drink together tonight.'

'We'll see,' said Lady LaToya, already pulling Nico Min away with her. 'Come on, we don't want to disturb these people any longer; every minute costs a fortune.'

She wanted to get back to the moped as quickly as possible and race off. She'd found the incident alarming. It was a warning of the unreality of her experiences, the untrustworthy theatricality of them. It must be an omen.

'Fantastic, isn't it?' said Nico Min when he was finally facing forwards. 'Nobody's dead.'

Green branches with pink blossom had woven themselves into the net above Bambi's terrace. There was a net stretched across Bambi's hair, too; as a chef he probably wore it to make a hygienic impression. Hard at it with a large saucepan, he nodded to them from the kitchen window, which looked out onto a tiny courtyard with small turquoise tables. Lady LaToya and Nico Min waved.

'Jorgos!' Bambi shouted angrily.

A slim boy sauntered through the shell curtain holding two menus. It didn't escape LaToya's attention that he straightened his shoulders, that something changed in his face as soon as he saw Nico Min. The words 'close by' occurred to her.

'What is it?' asked Nico Min.

She raised her eyebrows quizzically, with a carefree smile. A falcon, she thought. A bird of prey.

'My son!' Bambi exclaimed.

Bambi junior handed them each a menu—provocatively polite, LaToya thought—and told them he'd caught the octopus today. It didn't come any fresher than that.

Nico Min asked him something in Greek. With Bambi senior he'd spoken English, so that LaToya could understand. A painful tightness took hold of the inside of her skull. She played with her ring. Bambi junior's teeth were surprisingly large and straight. He didn't look at her once. They exchanged a few sentences, laughed about something with boyish cordiality and then he went back indoors.

'What were you talking about?' It took her a lot of effort to make her voice sound normal, but she felt she'd brought it off rather well. See it as a test, she thought. Please see it as a test.

'I asked him whether he really had caught the octopus himself and he said I could choose whether or not to believe him.'

'What's so funny about that?' She sniffed.

Startled, he stared at her in bewilderment.

Supercilious innocence, thought Lady LaToya, never lost, never lonely, never left with nothing. She was becoming trapped. Along with the wind, evil spirits had come down out of the hills. They'd escaped the sulphur and got inside her. She needed to find a way to drive them out or they'd take over, control her, speak through her mouth.

'So I went ahead and ordered the octopus,' said Nico Min—guiltily, LaToya felt. What was the next step? So I merely gave the boy a blow job? She had to think about something else. The food. What she wanted to eat.

'I've been looking forward to souvlaki all day,' she whined.

He went to set things right immediately, walking to the kitchen window. Bambi senior told them unequivocally that it wasn't a problem at all.

She stood with her back to him and knew he wasn't so close without a reason. He wanted her to turn to face him so she could wipe everything away with kisses, simple explanations if necessary: stomach cramps, tiredness. But she kept her lips firmly together for fear of what might escape them.

'I have the feeling I irritate you,' he said. 'Since this evening.'

The waves smashed viciously against the rocks.

'I can tell that you never had to think. Never had to do anything.'

A little air escaped his lips. After that he seemed to give up breathing.

Blasted in the bud, thought Lady LaToya. Stay here. Leave me in peace.

'I'll sleep in my own room tonight,' he said. 'Then you can find out whether you miss me.'

I miss you already, thought LaToya, but she nodded, casting her eyes down as she kissed him beside his lips, then climbed the stairs without looking back.

In her room they were waiting for her, the ghosts from

174

the volcano. They pressed her face into the pillow, from one cheek to the other, filling her head with sentences. He just wanted to try out a transvestite for once. He foresaw all this. You're reacting according to plan. Someone's waiting for him. Bambi junior takes him to a beach. You can't find it, no matter how hard you search. It's not going quickly enough for Nico Min. You've not seen him like this. He slaps the hands away, undoes his trousers himself, doesn't think about hovering. His hips in the wet sand. Four trembling young man's legs. 'Does your mother let you do this?' asks Bambi junior. Nico Min bursts out laughing, understanding the joke. The mother, that's you.

Lady LaToya looked at the impression in the pillow, the shroud of a clown. No, no, she thought, out of the question. In the bathroom she started to repair the damage. His wings had slid to the floor, she noticed over the shoulder of her mirror image.

He wasn't in his room, nor in the hotel bar. The receptionist asked Lady LaToya not to shout like that, the guests were free, they could do as they liked.

Get even with him. Make up for it. She would go into the village, towards the noise, the music, that's what he must have done, to dance, to hunt. The square with the big tree was filling with people, none of whom looked familiar. Small glasses were being handed round. LaToya took one from a tray and tossed it back. A tousled woman laughed at her, gave LaToya her own glass and laughed even louder when she immediately downed that one as well. It looked as if the woman had already had a good bit herself. This must be the local alcoholic; LaToya could smell it. She described Nico Min in English, but the woman slurred back at her in Greek—painful episodes in her youth, perhaps, that sent her into a trance. LaToya took a cigarette from her. It was years since she'd smoked. In combination with the little glasses, it was an enjoyable activity. She knocked back another four before the cigarette was finished.

Then she saw Jorgos, Bambi junior. He was standing talking with a girl, a cover.

'Where is he?' said Lady LaToya. The girl looked at her, startled. Bambi junior seemed to find it amusing.

'Did you two have a fight?' he asked.

She wanted to throw a full tray of glasses in his face, to drown him in the sea.

'I don't know where he is.' His self-imposed patience, some aggression already lurking—he was lying, he had to lie. Arms crossed, she stood there. He tried to go on talking with the girl, but the conversation flagged because the child continued to stare at LaToya, genuinely frightened. Bambi junior said something about a bit of privacy. The people around them started looking in her direction, ready to intervene.

To keep herself under control she went in search of a toilet. On the way the alcoholic handed her another glass. It could be some other boy, it could be anyone. The bodies pressed even more tightly together, making a circle around a fat man who, bending forward, was staggering slowly from left to right, arms outstretched. The music had grown louder, a voice accompanied by a bouzouki, a voice full of poetic pain, misfortune, hurt pride, fatalistic insights, impassioned cynicism, torment, bad tidings, self-blame. His arms lifted higher, the man leaped and spun on his axis with astonishing vitality, gracefully virile, his face averted. Leave me in peace. Stay here.

Approving cries, applause; from all sides people tossed paper napkins that fluttered down over the dancer.

'Aha. Look who's here!'

Lady LaToya quickly dabbed her tears. The director might already have noticed them. Not now, she thought.

'I got the fright of my life when you two walked into the frame,' he said. He seemed to have been drinking as well. 'What on earth is that, I thought. Carnival? Here?' He laughed loudly, quietening down after looking LaToya in the eye.

'Could it be that I saw your friend at the harbour?'

She pushed him aside, him and others, without offering any excuses. Her heels tapped rapidly along the footpath next to the sea. Shat-tered, shat-tered her steps and their echo whispered. He wouldn't have done anything to hurt himself, would he, her angel-boy, her sweet friend? She quickened her pace, stumbled, twisted her ankles. She reached the harbour out of breath. Not a single boat was moored there. He wasn't going to get away that easily.

The hotel. He was sure to be waiting there in her room. She climbed the stairs and inspected the empty space, the bathroom, even opened a cupboard. He'd taken his wings with him.

Lady LaToya flung back the shutters against the outside walls when she heard a speedboat.

'Stay here!' she shouted.

Destination

It was so long since Gregory Van Petegem last tasted freedom that the odd flavour of it surprised him. He did his best to keep an eye on both the winding road and the landscape on all sides. By taking in the grandeur surrounding him he'd been hoping to fulfil one of the minimal conditions of enjoying his recently acquired status. He felt that his failure to do so was the fault of the many bends up ahead, which kept distracting him from the landscape and made him feel nervous and uncertain.

He was now a person looking for solutions to the inconveniences he would once have called problems, so he decided to turn off onto the next open space at the side of the road that looked suitable for parking. That meant driving further than he'd initially thought. He got out, ran to the far side of the road, pressed himself up against the crash barrier, closed his eyes, breathed in through his nose and out through his mouth, and tried to make himself as receptive as possible.

The landscape was a carpet of round-breasted sleeping women in green dresses.

He must hold onto that thought, Gregory decided. With as much interest as he could muster, he watched the wind blowing through the tops of the trees. Unfortunately the spectacle didn't make him think of giants breathing deeply and reassuringly in their sleep; instead the wind seemed more like an agile rat hunting in vain for a way out from beneath their green frocks.

Slaloming to the accompaniment of a fanfare of shrill metallic noises, a sporty jeep hobbled across with a flat tyre and hammered into the crash barrier beside him. It folded like plasticine not quite dry enough to break.

If he hadn't watched with his own eyes as a bashful boy clambered out of the wrecked vehicle, Gregory would never have imagined he might be the driver. He looked sixteen at the most, blond and very pale—although you could perhaps put the paleness down to the circumstances.

'Sorry. *Excusez-moi*. What are you doing here anyway?' the boy whimpered with a German accent.

'You didn't hit me,' said Gregory.

'I skidded. A patch of oil or something. Dammit. My tyre.' Perhaps he was from Limburg rather than Germany. A Limburger in Luxembourg; that was possible. His blue eyes filled with tears. 'It's my mother's car.'

Then he stared at the landscape. The tears kept rising without falling overboard. Just let them drop, thought Gregory with concern, before trying to work out what the boy was looking at.

The rat went on running.

'Beautiful, eh?' was all Gregory said.

The crash barrier and the view stretched for miles. He felt vaguely responsible for the boy. There was no reason at all to go on standing so close to each other, gazing in this direction, car crash or otherwise.

Gregory turned round when a camper van approached.

For a moment he saw the driver's face, on which astonishment made way for an accusatory frown, as if the boy, or he, had deliberately parked a car in a bent crash barrier to deny camper van drivers part of the roadway. On the white flank of the passing holiday home it said, in blue letters, SEA, SAND & SUN. The boy's round cheeks trembled for a moment along with the road. Other than that he just went on looking angrily at the landscape. Gregory imagined him falling, this young man, off the rocks and out of the treetops, jumping and falling and sustaining life-threatening injuries.

'Come on,' he said. 'We'll try moving your car and then go and get help.'

The sound produced by the jeep as Gregory drove it to the other side of the road suggested a waking jungle. Close to the Skoda it fell silent.

His passenger emitted resentful noises, wound down the window and thrust his phone as high into the air as possible. Gregory drove on in silence.

'Might we see a phone box somewhere?' the boy asked at last.

He said he thought so.

'Fuck. Fuck. Fuck.'

'No signal, then?' Gregory inquired cautiously.

'Obviously not!'

Anyone else would have called him rude, but Gregory Van Petegem sensed at once that the boy had an affliction that mainly turned itself against him. His travelling companion stuck his left thumb in his mouth and started biting bits off an already very short nail. There were scars on the back of his hand. An observation about them was probably not the best way of breaking the silence. What did Gregory know about scars? He couldn't guess either their age or the depth of the wounds that had caused them. To him scars were illegible handwriting. He knew they came in all shapes and sizes, of course. Kitten claws could inflict them during play, as could recently sharpened, poorly aimed ninja stars, or a penknife. And the kinds of pain they reminded you of could vary greatly.

'Do you have a penknife?' he asked.

'Why?'

I've got a little thing here on my dashboard that I want to pick at with a knife.

The boy looked suspiciously at the dashboard and Gregory felt a fool. It was a pristine dashboard and it probably didn't matter whether the boy had a knife. 'I'll take a look in a bit,' he said before the boy could answer and then, happy to have thought of it at last: 'What's your name, by the way? I'm Gregory.'

'Jake.' The boy sank back a little in the seat.

'Sheik? That's a very unusual name. Or is it short for something? A nickname?'

'J-A-K-E.'

'Oh, Jake!'

'That's what I said.'

'Yes. Sorry. Cool.'

Cool was a word that didn't suit Gregory, which was why it hovered for so long in the car.

They passed a sign that told them the closest village was two kilometres away.

'We're sure to find a phone there.'

'Don't you have one?' Jake asked fiercely. It was plain that he assumed Gregory was deliberately withholding a mobile.

'No,' said Gregory. 'I've liberated myself from it.'

Jake's thoughts seemed to get stuck somewhere between contempt and incredulity. The accompanying facial expression drew a brief smile from Gregory. He turned smoothly off onto the even more winding road that led to the village. 'A young guy like you probably wouldn't understand that. Life without a mobile phone. Without a laptop or internet. I'll explain it to you.'

'Don't bother,' said Jake.

Gregory leaned on the bonnet of the car while Jake made the call. Here the green hills surrounded quiet streets. At a window in one of the silent house fronts a girl of about twelve stood looking at him. She was wearing a bikini. Gregory gave her a friendly nod, even waved briefly, but the girl's mouth remained a straight line. Gregory didn't want to think about today's youth. On reaching forty-seven last month he'd suddenly felt very old, but he must never become bitter. A young girl like that was no more representative of her generation than Jake, who was now using the receiver as a hammer. He alternated his hacking with angry kicks to the phone-box door. The boy must be dealing with a serious trauma if this was the effect of a phone call to his mother. Caution was called for here. And the timely provision of clarity. Life had taught Gregory that.

'If your mother can't pick you up, I could give you a lift.'

Jake looked at him like a cornered animal, an animal with

a large amount of blood pumping in its head.

'She's probably busy,' said Gregory. 'It doesn't matter that you're crying.'

Barely comprehensible through all the snot and sniffling, Jake roared that he wasn't crying, that his mother had fuck all to do, except for riding horses and screwing her latest victim in a five-star Luxembourg hotel, and that, as she saw it, if he could wreck her four-wheel-drive he could get it fixed as well. She'd called him an adult for the first time and refused point-blank to come and fetch him.

'Come on,' said Gregory. 'We'll look for a garage to take care of the car and then I'll drive you home.'

'I'm not going back to my mother,' said Jake.

Gregory didn't want to ask what the boy was planning to do in that case. If Jake said what Gregory expected him to say—that he'd hang himself from the nearest branch strong enough to take his weight—then everything would suddenly become pretty extreme. It was often better to leave things unsaid and to be proactive—Gregory remembered that from a course on business management, which admittedly had nothing to do with suicide but seemed applicable in virtually all situations. 'First the garage,' he said.

They drove past the house with the girl. Jake wound down the window on the passenger side and shouted 'Whore!'

The girl sucked her middle finger before sticking it up at them.

The garage owner was enjoying his well-earned Sunday rest, grumbled about wrecked knees and was expecting visitors, or so Gregory divined from the man's peculiar French. The chances of persuading him to repair the jeep appeared negligible and when Gregory realized the man was sloshed to the eyeballs as well he resigned himself.

Jake found that rather more difficult. After pacing up and down the forecourt with his jaws clamped together he threatened to snap the windscreen wiper off a vintage car.

'Your son's crazy,' the man said.

Gregory wasn't sure whether he should deny any family connection. Shouting that the boy had nothing to do with him wouldn't just sound like betrayal, it would be a lie.

As he stood contemplating this dilemma, Jake snapped off the windscreen wiper and threw it to the ground next to the vintage car with a childishly challenging gesture.

'Jake, don't do that,' said Gregory.

Swearing, and with no trace of knee trouble, the man stormed into his garage. Hollow, metallic noises could be heard and the sound of a toolbox falling over.

'I think we'd better go.' Gregory bent down to pick up the severed car part, which he carefully laid on the bonnet of the polished vehicle—a Jaguar, he noticed. What would a windscreen wiper like that cost? A special model, an item that was no longer made but which a handful of people on this planet would fight over. Gregory took a fifty-euro note out of his wallet and clamped it between wiper and bonnet. It probably wasn't enough, but it was all he had on him.

'You're actually going to pay that moron?' Jake shouted. But he shrank away like a newborn rodent when the garage owner stormed back out and stuck a handgun in the air.

'*Dégage*,' said the man in a voice that sounded a lot deeper and more sober than it had a minute before.

The fact that Jake walked backwards towards the Skoda, the way he did, hands stretched out in front of him, reached it unharmed and allowed himself to be driven away without protest, convinced Gregory that fate had been averted for the time being and that in the best of all possible worlds, now, now, now, skidding round the bends of an endless hill road, there was no such thing as fate. What if Jake had provoked the garage owner into shooting him? What if he'd snatched the weapon and stuck the barrel in his own mouth? That hadn't happened.

They'd been driving south for half an hour when Gregory decided that he now really ought to ask a question. 'Where do you want to go? Shall I turn round and take you to your mother?'

'No.'

It was as if the boy's nail-biting had begun resonating somewhere in the back of Gregory's skull. The sound gave him goosebumps. Talking seemed better than biting, and because he wanted to be able to look at the boy as they talked, he drove on for a bit and then parked near some picnic tables.

'You dumping me here?' asked Jake.

'Of course not. Let's look for a solution together.'

'You a priest or something?'

Gregory smiled. He'd been asked that question before. He wasn't a priest. He had no calling of any kind any longer. The only thing he'd firmly believed was that a new destination would soon present itself. And now that had happened.

'Like to come with me?'

'For all I care you can dump me here. I don't give a hoot.'

There was something about the combination of the word 'hoot' and this dejected young ruffian that made Gregory feel like laughing out loud. He resisted the urge.

'It's getting dark. I suggest we look for a hotel. Then you can sleep on it,' he said gently.

Jake shrugged. Gregory started the engine.

The middle-aged couple who ran the bed and breakfast had just had a fight. Across the man's cheek ran the red print of half a hand. The woman was fanatically picking fluff off her sweater. When she instructed the man to take the ironed sheets upstairs, he answered 'Yes' far too loudly, and when she handed both Gregory and Jake a key he shouted furiously at her that perhaps she might have liked to ask the guests first whether they wanted two rooms.

'Two rooms are fine,' said Gregory.

His travelling companion made a dazed impression. 'I don't have any money on me,' he said sulkily as he followed Gregory up the stairs to the bedrooms.

'No problem,' said Gregory. 'Just go and shower. I'll knock when it's time to arrange something for dinner.'

He went into his own room and heard Jake on the other side of the wall already turning on the shower. He wasn't going to slash his wrists, was he? Fortunately there was no bath. Listening to the running water, Gregory took in the stone floor of his own bathroom, the lily-patterned pillows and the complicated chandelier.

The decor had a strange effect on him. The laugh he'd managed to suppress in the car now rolled through his body in towering waves. To prevent Jake from hearing him, he held one of the lily pillows to his mouth, which merely caused his nose to make long, tormented noises. His tears of laughter poured in all directions, his stomach muscles quaked in dismay at the unexpected effort. The garage man's contorted face, the voices of the man and woman downstairs, the boy on the other side of the wall, the wrecked jeep with night falling on it—this was a spasm, an attack of insanity, and it was doing him good, an inordinate amount of good. Gregory dried his face with the pillow and chuckled as he recovered.

When his face had regained its normal colour, he walked downstairs, knocked on the door to the living room and went in.

The woman stood ironing in front of the television, separated by a big glass sliding door from her husband who, in the rain, wearing an excessively warm anorak, was wildly trimming a hedge. Gregory bit his lower lip.

'My dear madam, I don't wish to disturb you, but do you know where we can find something to eat?'

The woman immediately discovered another bit of fluff on her sweater. 'The restaurant we always recommend is shut,' she said. 'There's a pita bread place in the village. Or do you want sandwiches? If sandwiches are enough I can bring you some up straight away. Goat's cheese and blueberry sandwiches? And crab salad. Crab salad? I'm sorry not to invite you down, but the atmosphere here isn't exactly uplifting, as you may have noticed.'

'Sandwiches are fine. And upstairs is fine too,' said Gregory. 'For the two of us, please. Me and the boy.'

Outside the man shook an insect out of the sleeve of his anorak.

Gregory went back upstairs and knocked on the door to Jake's room. There was no response. After he'd banged on the door with his fist only for the silence on the other side of the door to continue, he decided not to waste any time. He'd felt this coming; the laughing fit had distracted him. Fortunately the boy hadn't locked the door. Gregory stormed over to the bed and pulled Jake's limp body towards him by the shoulders.

'Jake!'

'What the hell is it?' Jake mumbled sleepily. The first eye he opened was instantly on full alert.

The laughing started again. With screeching howls Gregory pressed the boy to him. 'Sorry, sorry!' he squeaked between each one. Jake looked more and more frightened, which didn't make it any easier for Gregory to regain self-control. He let go of the struggling body and tried to calm himself.

'I'm so glad you're alive!'

'Creep,' said Jake.

'I keep thinking you're going to do yourself some kind of harm. I'm sorry.'

'Why would I do anything to myself?' Jake asked angrily.

'I'd understand if you did,' Gregory rattled on. 'Often it's difficult. One moment the cheese you make is the organic cheese of the year, the next you're responsible for fourteen employees losing their jobs. Life could at the very least be described as unsettled.'

'Don't touch me, please,' the boy said in measured tones.

Gregory took his hand off a knee. It occurred to him that his intentions had been misunderstood. He quickly tried to switch to an impersonal subject.

'Are you of age?' he asked.

'Too old for you,' the boy snarled.

'No!' Gregory exclaimed. 'I mean: do you have a driver's licence. Are you actually allowed to drive that car?'

'Out of my room, please.'

It seemed that when he really wanted his requests to be complied with, Jake became courteous.

'Sleep well,' said Gregory. 'If you want to go with me in the morning, I'm leaving at half past eight.'

On the landing between the doors to their rooms, a peculiar feeling came over him, a sense that he was in a bit of his life that he'd never forget. He walked on. I'm stronger than most people, he thought, more persistent than any assumptions.

He'd only just sat down on the edge of his own bed when the woman knocked. He took two trays of food from her and ate everything. Immediately after that he removed his clothes and laid his head in the valley between two lily pillows. He fell asleep instantly.

Jake didn't look at him at breakfast. His mouth full of bread, the boy asked if he could come along and Gregory replied that he'd take him to his mother. No protest followed.

They said nothing to each other on the way there, not even when they drove past the jeep. Around the wheels of the Skoda the puddles kept up their self-satisfied splashing. Summer was a long way off yet.

Just before getting out, Jake said Gregory could go to bed with him as long as he paid.

Gregory politely declined.

For more information or to receive our newsletter,
please contact us at: info@worldeditions.org.